CATS AND OTHER CREATURES

T. THORN COYLE

Hunting is joy. Blood on claw and tooth. The crunch of tiny bones. The sense of power.

But mostly, the focus. Stillness. Waiting. Stalking. Waiting. Collecting speed in muscles until...strike. Snap! Victory.

Even the occasional misses satisfy. They teach me other things I need to know. The arc of the trajectory. The inaccuracies in gauging speed.

All of these are fixable, with time.

A BRIEF INTRODUCTION FROM THE AUTHOR

Cats. Foxes. Spaniels. Faery. Fantasy. Science fiction...

These stories are filled with whimsy and possibility. They look at what happens in the places most humans never even think to look. The places animals know so well.

These are stories filled with the magic of surprise. They ask what life might be like if we sought past the ordinary.

The six tales are varied. I put this collection together to thank the backers of my Bookshop Witch Kickstarter. These stories are also dedicated to my amazing Patreon supporters, without whom most of them would not exist.

So here they are: revolutionary super-cats, murderous garden cats, faeries, strange visitations, cat detectives, and worlds beyond what we currently know.

Let's imagine them together.

T. Thorn Coyle
Portland, Oregon
2021

RHIANNON AND THE QUEEN OF CATS

Gnomes are ridiculous.

I was half-napping in the bookstore window, curled up against a stack of the latest urban fantasy novels, a sunbeam warming my face.

Then that witch, Delta Crabbit, walked in, tote bag stuffed with a cranky gnome. Not that I saw any of this, but Delta's voice carries, and the gnome's thrashing was pretty loud. Sigh. I settled back into my restful pose, hoping Delta and my human, Sarah, would have their little conversation, Delta would get the books she had on order, and then they would leave.

A cat can dream, can't she?

But it wasn't to be.

Since the only other person in the store was my witch, Sarah—and Biff the resident ghost didn't care—Delta decided the gnome could come out to play.

Great. Just great. That dang gnome loved nothing more than to bother me.

Sure enough…

"Pssst!" a gravely little voice said. "Hey! Cat! You awake?"

I opened one eye. And there, staring at me from behind a display of notebooks, were those shiny button eyes, ruddy cheeks, and white beard, all of it topped by a blue cap with purple stitching. The gnome. My nemesis. The bane of my existence.

Oh, he didn't know that. But I did. And what I know is the only thing that matters.

"Did you hear the news?"

Now, that got my attention. I opened both eyes and lifted my head.

"What news?"

"There's a new cat in town. Says she has magical powers. Says she's the real Justice in town. Not your witch."

I sat up and glared. "Where is this creature?"

"She sometimes holds court in that little parking lot behind Angie's cafe. I met her when I was visiting the greenhouse there."

Well, well, well. Wasn't this interesting? The scruff of my neck bristled.

"Show me," I said, leaping from the window display. I padded toward the door, then realize the gnome wasn't with me. Looking back, I saw him carefully attempting to climb down, stepping on stacks of books that teetered precariously, hopping onto a low bookcase. Finally, he made his way to the floor.

I stood at the door and yelled.

"Rhiannon?" Sarah asked. "You can't go out. You know that." Her pale brow furrowed in the way that meant she was questioning something. "You never go out."

"Preston, what are you doing?" Delta Crabbit's voice was as sharp as her eyes, peering at the gnome from beneath the wild tufts of her gray hair.

Huh. The gnome's name was Preston. I had no idea.

I turned to meow at Sarah, to reassure her everything was fine. She was right, though. I didn't go out. I preferred the cozy warmth of the bookstore—or her house—along with the free food and head scratches. But sometimes a cat has to do what a cat has to do. The door pushed open and the bells rang. Feet stepped toward me. A customer.

I darted past, and heard Sarah shout. The gnome was hot on my heels. We had to get away before the witches caught up. Luckily, a customer would slow Sarah down, and I didn't think Delta was all that fit.

The scent of briny sea air hit me along with the smells of popcorn and saltwater taffy and car exhaust. The slight tang of rotting fish provided an under note to the ocean breeze. My stomach growled. But I had no time to think of fish.

"Lead on," I said, ignoring Delta's muffled shouts from the sidewalk behind us. I had a vague idea where the café was, but the gnome knew the lay of the land. Once we'd gotten far enough away, I slowed down to match the pace of his stumpy legs. At this rate, it was going to take us hours to make it down the few blocks of Main Street, dodging tourists and locals alike.

The gnome turned off Main and led me toward a small parking area in what must have been the rear of Angie's cafe. Sure enough, I saw a glass structure with what looked like plants inside. The greenhouse.

And, holding court, with half a dozen cats and a squirrel or two gathered around her dainty paws, was a large cat with calico fur.

She stopped speaking and looked up at me with amber eyes. My own eyes narrowed, and I resisted the urge to hiss.

"You brought the Justice's minion, I see." She spoke to the gnome, but directed the words at me.

This time, I hissed.

"I am no one's minion." I stiffened my gait and stalked her way. The other cats backed off, clearly wanting to avoid a fight.

That was interesting. To my knowledge, outdoor cats were always sparring over something or another. What power did this interloper have?

The calico huffed at me. "If you are no one's minion, why are you not Justice of this town? Why let a witch do what a cat ought?"

What kind of fool question was that? I stopped and glared. "Because I already have a job in the bookshop. That keeps me in kibble, a warm bed, and as many head scratches as I desire. Why would I wish for more work?"

The other cats nodded.

"Makes sense to me," a slinky gray cat said to a marmalade tomcat beside her. The cat looked sad.

But sad or not, she was correct. No cat wants to work more than they need to.

I moved toward the group again, the gnome at my side. The sounds from the street faded, as did the rumble of waves from down the cliffs. A blue jay scolded high up in a spruce. We all ignored it, except one squirrel, which chittered back, until the marmalade cat swiped at it.

"Ridiculous!" the calico scoffed, then turned to the gnome. "Everyone wants power. Clearly this *cat...*" the calico spat the word. My hair rose at the insult, but the gnome poked my shoulder.

"Don't rise to the bait," he murmured.

We would see. But for now? I remained silent, and padded closer, eyes never leaving the calico's smug face.

"Clearly this cat does not have the power she claims." She was repeating herself, but I wouldn't point that out. Yet. "What cat with access to cat magic would not wish to wield power? What cat would not wish for humans to do their bidding, and other cats bow at their feet?"

I sat on my haunches and yowled out a laugh. "Humans already do my bidding, every day. And what need have I for other cats to bow? All cats are autonomous and anyone with the ability to think knows this. No cat shall ever be held in thrall."

The calico trained those amber eyes on me, as if

she could drill a hole into my skull. It was unnerving, I admit, but I held still and returned her gaze.

"You are a fool, then. And things in this town are going to change."

Then she stood, turned, and simply walked away.

The other cats looked from her to me, clearly confused.

"You are your own cats," I said. "Do not let someone tell you otherwise, no matter how beautiful or mean they are."

A few of the cats looked at me with interest, but others bowed their heads and slunk away.

"You cats are strange," one squirrel said.

It's little squirrel friend nodded. "Let's go get some juniper berries. They should be ripe."

The two squirrels bounded off in search of food.

The marmalade cat approached.

"You had best watch your back, my friend. That cat is up to no good. But as for me? Should you ever wish my company, this one knows where I live."

He nodded at the gnome, then bumped my shoulder with his own, and sauntered away.

"Wait!"

The marmalade tomcat stopped and looked back at me. He was a handsome brute.

"Did something happen? Something that needs a Justice?"

"Trixie's kitten has disappeared. The runt. It was

the last one left in the litter, and she had decided to raise it herself."

"When did this happen?" I assumed that Trixie was the sad looking gray cat who'd been sitting next to marmalade, here.

"Few nights ago," he shrugged. "I don't know much more about it, except that Trixie is upset. But like I said, you watch your back. And you need me? Send the gnome here to ask for Tom."

Really? His name was actually Tom? Some cats have no imagination. Not that I would ever tell a cat that. Especially not a handsome one.

"Thanks. I'll keep that in mind."

He nodded, blinked, then sauntered off between two garbage cans.

"How do you know all these cats?" I asked when we finally stood alone in the small parking lot again.

The gnome shrugged. "They like the café garbage. And I like Angie's double chocolate chip cookies and help with her plants. Besides, it's Delta's favorite spot, so we come here all the time."

Okay. I guess that made sense. Clearly there was a whole world outside the bookshop and I needed to start paying attention to it.

But what was next? What did it mean that a strange cat was in town, talking about being a Justice?

And where was Trixie's missing kitten?

I waited outside the bookshop door as the gnome hid in a bush. Two human men approached down the sidewalk. One pushed a baby in a stroller, the other held the chubby hand of a small child.

This was my chance. I meowed, then preened a bit in the sun. I knew it made my black fur look glossy and soft.

That was part of how I controlled humans. No magic needed, calico cat.

"Look!" said the child, black curls lifting in the ocean breeze, "a kitty!"

"Careful, sweetheart," said the man pushing the baby stroller.

The other man crouched next to the child. "Some kitties don't like to be touched. Remember what we said about asking?"

The child nodded. "Kitty? May I pet you?"

I bumped up against the tyke, who squeed, then softly patted my side with a chubby hand.

After a few moments of receiving the child's tribute, I backed off, and pawed at the door, meowing again.

"Daddy, it wants to go inside!"

The two men looked at each other. The crouching one stood and regained the child's hand.

Stroller human said, "Cats know where they belong."

That's right, human, we do. I meowed again.

"Let's go in and see if the cat lives here."

"Books! Books! Books" The child jumped up and down, little sandals slapping the sidewalk in excitement.

The two men laughed, and then one of them opened the door.

The bells jangled. I shot through.

"Rhiannon! There you are!" Sarah scooted around from behind the counter. "I was worried!"

She crouched to scratch my head as Delta Crabbit scowled. Uh oh. The gnome was still outside. I jerked my head. Delta seemed to understand. She scurried toward the door, empty tote bag swinging. I enjoyed Sarah's attention for a moment longer, then ran down the center aisle between two bookcases. I needed to talk to Biff.

I heard Sarah thanking the two men for bringing me back, but had no time for their reply.

"Biff!"

The ghost appeared in front of me, hovering near the parapsychology section. He hung out there a lot, and I was never certain if it was some sort of ghost joke or if he'd been interested in the subject while alive.

"What do you need, cat?"

That brought me up short. What did I need from the bookshop ghost? I heard the gnome huffing behind me. He'd gotten away from Delta.

"The cat needs to know everything there is about cat magic and why a cat would want to become a Justice," Preston said.

"Also, there's a missing kitten." Both the gnome and the ghost looked at me. I shrugged. "Don't look at me. It's just part of the picture, here. I have no clue if the two are related."

Biff looked thoughtful and grew a bit more solid. A shaft of sun from one of the high windows shimmered as it hit him, illuminating the bookshelves behind him. A yellow spine caught my attention. I padded toward it, head craned to look.

"Hey! Watch where you're going!"

I stiffened and backed my nose out of cold ghost pant legs. "Sorry Biff!"

Even I knew it was the height of rudeness to walk through a ghost as if they were not there.

Biff harrumphed, but let it go. "What do you see, cat?"

"That yellow book. There." I pointed with my chin.

"Hmmm...." Biff levitated the book off the shelf. "The folklore section."

Biff threw the book on the floor. He does that. A lot. The bells on the shop door rang, and a child's voice raised, thanking Sarah for the books. The door shut.

Seconds later, two sets of feet raced down the aisle to the back of the shop.

"What in the nine worlds is going on back here?" Sarah demanded, dark eyes snapping, wavy black hair escaping from its makeshift bun.

I meowed and the gnome and I both shifted our bodies in front of the book that lay splayed on the wood planks of the floor.

"Preston!" Delta stomped on the floor. "What are you hiding there?"

I lay down flat on the book, but my black fur didn't quite cover the yellow cover.

"You had better not crack that spine," Sarah said, bending down to scoop me up. "Biff is hard enough on the books without you smashing them open."

I squirmed in her arms, but she held tight. The gnome moved to sit on the book, but Delta collared him.

"No." Sarah looked me dead in the eyes. "You're going to tell us what is going on. All of you. And that means you, too, Biff."

I yowled and squirmed some more.

"You aren't getting out of this that easily, Rhiannon. Use your words. I know you can talk."

She loosened her arms for a moment and I leapt free to the floor. Sarah sighed, and bent to pick up the battered yellow book.

"The King of Cats," she said. "What's this all about?"

I blinked at the witch, flummoxed. How did Sarah know I could talk?

And what did an old fairy tale have to do with anything?

The bells rang, signaling customers.

"Don't think we're done with this," Sarah said, then turned on her heel and headed toward the front of the bookshop.

Delta Crabbit plopped down in a comfy upholstered chair in the back corner, yellow book in hand. Biff had disappeared again, leaving the gnome and I to deal with the witch. How convenient for him. Dang ghost.

I sauntered toward the middle aisle.

"No you don't," Delta said. "You and Preston are going to tell me what is happening, and you're going to do it now. Before Sarah gets back."

Preston climbed onto one arm of the chair. I sighed, and sat a few feet away from Delta.

"There's a missing kitten," Preston began, "and an interloper. A power hungry cat."

The witches seemed remarkably unconcerned about the affairs of cats, insisting it had nothing to do with them, and that there was no way a cat could become Justice anyway, so what did it matter? And the kitten had probably wandered off.

Or gotten eaten by a coyote.

All of this added up to one thing...

I bobbed along in Delta's tote bag, a stowaway, trying to avoid the gnome's boots.

"Ouch!" I grumbled. He'd just poked me in the eye with that dang pointy cap of his.

"Scoot over," he hissed.

As if I could. The canvas of the sack was suffocating, and I really didn't like not being able to see what was going on. Let alone being trapped in a small space with a cranky gnome.

But it was the only way to get me out of the shop and back to the café. Delta went there every day, Preston had said, for coffee and sweets. There was nothing to eat in the café for cats, as far as I could tell, but it would get me closer to the alley, and that's what we needed.

The tote bag paused. I felt a jerk. Then the scents of sugar, cinnamon, and coffee tickled my nose. I sneezed.

"What?" Uh oh. That was Delta talking. Sure enough, the top of the bag opened, and her pale brown eyes peered down at me. I grabbed the canvas and clawed my way up, stepping on the gnome.

"Watch it!"

I leapt from my precarious perch and darted between legs, not heeding people's exclamations or Delta, shouting after me.

How did I get to the alley from there? The place was confusing. People everywhere. Table legs. A strange hissing noise. Music. Chatter.

"There's a cat!"

"Catch it!"

I doubled back and ran behind a long counter.

"Rhiannon? What are you..." Angie. She came into the bookshop sometimes. No time to stop. I careened past hot ovens, past the big metal sink, heading toward the back. There had to be a door here, right?

I barreled through the kitchen, claws scrabbling on the floor, heading toward a wedge of light. A propped open door. Yes!

Bursting through, I almost crashed into a Dumpster.

Delta and the gnome were waiting for me.

"You foolish cat," Delta said. "Why didn't you just tell me you needed to get back here? I would have spoken with Sarah about it."

As if. The witches had made it quite clear they wanted nothing to do with cat problems.

She rubbed her shoulder. "I wondered why Preston's bag was so heavy."

The gray cat slinked forward, looking dejected.

"Have you come to find my kitten?"

"You're Trixie, right?"

The gray cat nodded.

"I'm Rhiannon. Can you tell us what happened?"

She led us toward the greenhouse, then further, toward the towering spruces just beyond. The trees separated the small parking lot from a house next door. A dilapidated, weathered wood fence showed a gap between two boards.

"My human lives in that house. All my kits were adopted out except..." she stopped, sniffed, and wiped a paw across her face.

"Except?" I prompted.

"Except for Bluebell. The smallest. My human decided we could keep her. She's the softest, sweetest little gray and white..."

"Okay, we get it," Preston said.

I glared up at the gnome, who was riding on one of Delta's shoulders. Guess he liked the view.

Turning back to Trixie, I gentled my voice. "When did Bluebell disappear?"

"Two nights ago. Everything was bright. The full moon, you know. So many cats were out and about, and Bluebell wanted to hear the singing."

A lot of cats did like to sing under the full moon. Well. Sing and fight... and other things. What can I say? It gets the blood up, a good full moon. Gives a cat the zoomies.

Delta crouched down, and the gnome clambered to the asphalt, then joined me on the prickly carpet of fallen spruce needles near the fence.

"Did she wander off? Or did somebody take her?"

"Someone took her," a new voice replied.

Our heads all whipped back toward the parking lot, and there, standing proudly between two compact cars was the marmalade. Tom.

"What did you see?"

He walked closer, broad shoulders swaying as he came. Get a grip, Rhiannon. First of all, you're fixed. Second of all…

"Could you say that again?" Oops. Way to miss some vital information.

The gnome poked me. "Pay attention, cat!"

"It was that new cat. The one who thinks she should be Justice."

"She took the kitten?" Delta asked.

Tom shook his head. "Not took, exactly. She has some sort of magic I do not know. She uses it against other cats, and some of the other smaller creatures, too."

The fur rose along my spine.

What had I said to that arrogant cat? *No cat shall live in thrall.* "She's using coercion to manipulate cats into doing her bidding."

And a worse thing than that? I couldn't imagine. Cats were meant to be sovereign and free.

"Sounds like a sort of glamour," Delta chimed in. "A nasty one."

"I don't care what it is," sniffed Trixie. "I just want my Bluebell back! I need to know that she's safe. And I want to know what you're going to do about this, Justice."

Everyone was looking at me. Even Delta.

"I… I'm not Justice here! That's Sarah! I'm just a cat."

Tom rumbled, then spoke. "You are the closest thing we have, Rhiannon. It is your job to sort this out. Why do you think we sent the gnome to get you?"

To get me. Not Sarah. Not a witch.

Me.

Great. Just great.

"Show me where she disappeared."

The investigation didn't tell me much. A few tufts of fur that could belong to Bluebell and the calico, but could also belong to any number of cats that passed between the cottage yard and the parking lot garbage cans and Dumpster.

Maybe that yellow book Biff had thrown would yield more information. So Delta, Preston, and I all headed back to the shop, leaving Tom to comfort Trixie.

That last part didn't sit right with me, but what's a cat gonna do?

At least I was walking this time, weaving past people, following Delta's lead. I had to dodge a few insistent children and one older woman, but made it back to the bookshop unscathed. Difficult as Seashell Cove's Main Street was to navigate on foot, it beat riding in Delta's canvas sack. How and why the gnome put up with it, I didn't know.

No way was I getting back into that sack again. Ever.

"Kitty kitty kitty kitty!" Uh oh. It was the toddler from before. The one with two dads.

"You're back out?" Stroller Dad said. "I thought you weren't allowed."

"Kitty!" The toddler's cloud of dark hair was even wilder than before, and ice cream drips decorated her chin. I never got ice cream. Sarah said it would make me sick.

I think she lies.

"I'm taking the rapscallion back to the bookshop," Delta assured the man. He looked skeptical. I didn't blame him. Her gray hair stuck up at odd angles, her tote bag was thrashing, and she had a weird gleam in her eye.

I sauntered up and stuck myself to her leg, as if to confirm.

The two men looked at each other and shrugged.

"Well, as long as someone is taking her where she belongs," said the other man, barely restraining the toddler from grabbing my tail. "Let the kitty alone, sweetie, it has places to be."

"And so do we," said Stroller Dad. The baby in the stroller kicked its little legs and cooed.

"Well then," Delta said, then walked on. I followed as closely as I could without tripping the witch.

"Hey!" Stroller Dad's voice stopped us. "We saw a kitten a little while ago. Were you out looking for it?"

A kitten.

Delta got very still. So did the gnome. So did I.

"Where did you see this kitten?" Delta asked.

"Behind the tamale parlor. After we had lunch," said the other man. "Right sweetie?"

"Right!" The toddler turned her big, dark eyes on me. "They told me I couldn't keep it, but they told the lady in the restaurant."

"Mrs. Vargas?" Delta asked.

"I guess so."

"Okay. Thank you!"

Delta whirled, almost whacking a woman carrying a rolled up kite. The woman scowled, but our strange trio raced up the sidewalk, back to the Widening Gyre.

Delta burst through the bookshop door with a clatter of bells. I barely made it inside.

We stopped short. There were customers in the store. A lot of them. Sarah shook her head, then jerked her chin toward the back of the shop. Again.

I looked longingly at the front display window, where a sunbeam played across the bright book covers. I really wanted a nap. I mean, cats are built to nap for eighty percent of the day, right?

This was turning into a very long day, and I had that dang calico to blame for it. She had interrupted my napping schedule, and she would pay.

Near the back of the store, Biff faded in and out, clearly excited about something. The yellow book sat on the comfy corner chair.

Delta picked up the book, set the tote bag on the chair, and the gnome climbed out, sputtering.

"Get a cushion or something for the bottom of the bag. It isn't very comfortable!"

Delta ignored him and began flipping through the yellow tome. "It says here that the King of Cats gathers subjects around him. The more his power grows, the more other animals flock to him."

"But that calico cat is female," the gnome began.

Delta and I both stared. He wisely shut his tiny rosebud mouth and stroked his long white beard.

"Just like with witches or warlocks, sex and gender don't matter," Delta said, voice dry. "What matters is..."

"This is a cat who wants to rule," I said. And that wasn't good at all.

Conveniently, Vargas's Tamale Parlor was located next door to the bookshop. After she finished with the customers, Sarah put a "Back in Fifteen Minutes" sign up and locked the door.

"I texted Duncan. He'll be back from his break in ten," she said. Duncan was the store manager when Sarah wasn't around. I liked him. He gave me treats.

We walked from the bookshop's tiny parking lot to the much larger one behind the restaurant. I hadn't been outside this much in years. My paws were sore from walking on concrete and gravel. Wood floors and carpeting are much more my jam.

I walked toward the garden around the building. The plants were tended by chaneques, short stocky Fae beings as tall as a couple of gnomes. One of them came out from behind a rock to greet us. He had a blocky face and light brown skin and dark hair. Soil covered his clothing, and he was signing something.

"I'm so sorry, friend, I don't understand," Delta began, right as a second chaneque emerged.

This one held a purring, blue-eyed kitten in its arms.

"Bluebell?" I asked, padding quickly across dirt and sand, slinking my way between rocks and plants.

"Who are you?" the kitten squeaked.

"My name is Rhiannon. These are the witches Delta and Sarah, and Preston, the gnome."

"Sarah? Rhiannon? Like the Justices?"

Sarah shot me a look, but nodded. "Yes. I'm the Justice in Seashell Cove, and Rhiannon is my familiar."

I glared back. Way to downgrade my importance in front of another cat, Sarah. I mean, sure, I'd told the other cats I wasn't Justice, but...

"How did you get here?" Delta asked. "Your mother is worried."

The kitten nodded gravely. "I know. But I had to try to stop the calico cat. She is bad for all cat kind."

Ain't that the truth, kitten.

"How did you know?" I asked.

"She tried to kidnap me. I bit her arm and she smacked me on the nose. Hard." The kitten sneezed. "After that, I told her I would come and pretended she'd hypnotized me. But... she hooked me all the same. Like the others. I mean, I feel kind of funny. Maybe she did it when I was asleep?"

Bluebell looked confused, but there was no time to figure out exactly what she meant by all of that.

"What others?" Sarah asked.

The first chaneque signed something, then turned and motioned for us to follow.

We moved through the garden, past a large stone cairn that must be the entrance to the chaneques' home. Finally, we were at a drop off covered with rocks and plants. It leveled out to another garden.

And at the base of a Japanese maple tree sat the calico, surrounded by cats and a few squirrels. Strangely, two white seagulls perched on a rock nearby, nattering to each other. I wouldn't think a cat would have any sway over them.

"Bluebell!" The calico cat looked pleased. "You have brought friends! Though I thought I told you no humans."

Sarah stepped forward. I stayed at her side. "I'm not a human, cat. I'm a witch."

"Oho! You are the one they call the Justice, are you not?"

"What's with talking like you're in an old book?" I said.

Calico pinned me with her eyes as if I was a mouse. Yeah. That didn't work on me.

She sniffed. "I'm sure I don't know what you mean. Have you come to swear fealty? And has the witch decided to lay the mantle of Justice upon my shoulders?"

I swear, the dang cat practically preened, as if someone had offered her a velvet cushion and a crown.

"No," Sarah replied. "We've come to demand you release these creatures from your thrall."

The calico laughed. "I assure you, every creature gathered is here of their own volition."

But I could see that was not true. Now that I knew to look for it, if I narrowed my eyes, I could see thin silver filaments that tied the surrounding creatures to the calico cat. Except the seagulls. Huh. They must just be here for their own amusement then. Must be a boring day on the coastline.

"Sarah." I spoke softly. It still felt strange to speak to a non-cat this way, but since she knew, I may as well. "She tied them to her."

I felt her breathing change, the way it did when she was about to do some witchy business.

"So I see," she murmured. "Delta?"

"I see it, too."

"Rhiannon, I'm Justice, but this is your call."

I sat for a moment. The calico yammered on, pontificating about something or other. I couldn't bother to care. I just needed…

There. I found where the silver threads wound themselves together into two slender ropes. One formed a chain of office around the calico's throat, and the other wound into a crown upon her head.

"She's feeding off them, in order to be queen."

"Nothing of the sort!" the calico cried. "I am queen, and therefore they wish to serve me."

"We'll just see about that," I said. "Sarah?"

Sarah looked at me, dark hair flowing around her shoulders. She was a tall one, the witch of mine. She appeared to be weighing something. Considering.

"As Justice of Seashell Cove, it is my job to make sure that justice is actually served, not only something that *calls* itself justice."

Everyone waited. Even the nattering seagulls were quiet.

Sarah looked at the calico, then back to me. "It seems pretty clear that you're the one who needs to make this decision, Rhiannon. You are the one with ties to the cat community and magical communities, both. It's your call, and I'll back you up."

Well then. I hadn't expected that.

I listened to the coastal wind for a moment. Tuned in again to the silvery cords binding cats and squirrels to the calico who would be queen.

"Bluebell?"

The kitten squeaked, but sat up at attention. The silvery cord binding her to the calico was slender and a bit frayed. Clearly, the kitten had been fighting the calico this whole time. Good.

"Are you willing to let me snap the tether binding you to this cat?"

"Yes, please!" Bluebell trembled with excitement. "What do I need to do?"

"Just sit still, and imagine a silver cord snapping. Sarah and I will do the rest."

The kitten nodded and closed her eyes. I looked at Sarah. She nodded, too.

"On your count," Sarah said.

"One." I took in a deep breath of sea air.

"Two." I focused on the silvery cord.

"Three!" With my mind, I snapped the cord in half. It let go with a flare of magic. The calico yelped as if stung. Bluebell shook herself, then opened her eyes.

"It worked! I can breathe properly again!" The little cat tumbled and laughed.

The other cats looked shocked.

"How dare you?" The calico sputtered.

Ignoring her, I scanned the group of cats and

squirrels. "This cat has done what no cat should ever do. She has tied you to her, against your will. If you wish to be freed from her tether, I will help you. Then, if you still choose to follow her? It will be a true choice, one you have made yourself, not one forced upon you."

Tom's voice sounded from behind me. "They do not understand."

I turned. He stood next to Trixie, who was busily licking Bluebell's head. When had they arrived?

"Oh, but we do," said a white cat with a dark smudge above her nose. "At least in theory. It is difficult to tell whether or not this one speaks truth, but there is a simple way to find out."

The white cat looked around. "If we allow this one, this Justice, to do what she will, there is no risk to us. Either it works, and we are free, or it is simply an illusion in her mind, and we continue as we are. We are free in either case, so I see no harm in it."

A murmuring arose among the cats. The squirrels chattered and the seagulls resumed their nattering.

"You have no authority here!" the calico cried.

"Neither do you," I replied. "What is your decision, cats and other friends?"

Well, calling the squirrels friends was a stretch, but they didn't need to know that. Not now, at any rate.

The cats looked to one another. I noticed they

avoided the eyes of the calico, whose tail thrashed in anger.

The white cat seemed to take their silence for assent. "We shall do as you suggest then."

Not one cat said a word. The seagulls leaned forward. Two squirrels clutched at one another with their tiny paws.

"Close your eyes," I said. "Imagine the silver cords that tie you to the calico cat. On the count of three, imagine those cords snapping in two. Ready?"

Silence. But all the creatures closed their eyes. Except the gulls, who watched with keen interest.

Okay then. "One."

I looked at Sarah. "Two." We said the word together.

"Three!" With a mighty yank, the cords all flared and snapped. Several cats fell, others whooped in delight.

The calico cat looked ashen. Her fur, once so glossy, was dull as dust. Her amber eyes dimmed.

She looked old.

The younger cats raced and played. Some of the older cats though? They looked upon the calico with anger.

"Justice!" Tom raised his voice above the clamor. "We demand justice! Look what she has done. To *cats!*"

That stopped the playing cats in their tracks.

Every cat turned to look at me. The calico stifled a sob.

"Is your freedom not enough?"

"Not if she can do this again," Sarah murmured.

Dang. The witch was right. "So what now?"

"Your call." She shrugged.

I never thought I would rue hearing those words again. Maybe I didn't want to be a Justice after all.

What would be a fitting sentence for the cat who would be queen?

"Cat," I stared into her eyes. There was no defiance left in them. Wasn't that punishment enough? But no. I saw a slight spark. A smirk she quickly wiped from her mouth. She was pretending. Not the aging part, that was clearly true, but she still plotted something, deep inside. A cat doesn't change its markings that swiftly, just as my mother said.

Delta and the gnome stepped forward. Huh. I'd half forgotten they were even there.

"I have mice," Delta said. "In my cottage."

Brilliant.

"Calico cat," I began.

"My name is Queenie." She drew herself up.

The other cats snorted and laughed.

"Not anymore, it isn't," the white cat said. "Perhaps your name should be Spot."

The calico hissed and spat.

I raised a paw for silence.

"Calico cat," I continued, "you shall live with the

witch Delta Crabbit and keep her cottage free of mice. You shall answer to a use name that you and the witch find suitable. And…"

I imagined a soft blanket settling across the calico's shoulders. It would not hurt her, but would muffle any future magic she attempted.

"You are forbidden to use magic against any other creature, for as long as you shall live. Do you understand?"

The calico gave a curt nod, but said nothing. The calculation I had seen before was gone.

"Is this sentence acceptable to you all?"

"It is to me," the white cat said.

The other cats voiced their assent. The squirrels had already run off to do their squirrely things.

Delta and the gnome collected the calico, who didn't put up much of a fight.

The chaneques climbed the hill back to their garden, and the other cats slowly dispersed, talking as they went.

"Thank you so much," Trixie said.

"Yes! Thank you, Rhiannon! You're the best cat, ever!"

I smiled down at the kitten. "You were very brave to fight her, Bluebell."

Trixie and Bluebell turned to Tom.

"Will you escort us home?" Trixie asked.

"I would be glad to." Then he looked at me. "Well done. Come and see me sometime?"

I nodded, unable to speak. He bumped me with his shoulder, then the three cats went on their way.

"Good work," Sarah said. "I think there's a tin of the fancy wet food at home. It has your name on it."

Thank the Cat Gods. I needed a good wash, some good food, and the softest cushion in Sarah's house.

And hopefully tomorrow? It would be a quiet day at the bookshop.

This had all been quite exciting, but a cat really needs her rest.

A Seashell Cove Paranormal Short Story.
Written for the
Bookshop Witch Kickstarter.

THE STARS OF NEVERWHERE

Who was going to save Samuel Lee?

That was where he was in the current story.

Things had grown so strange, he honestly didn't

know if he could take it anymore. The stack of library books piled on the floor wasn't helping. Neither was his favorite playlist.

All he could do was return to the story inside his head. The one he'd been making up since he was seven and a half and the strange man had moved in next door. Samuel was ten now.

The man seriously creeped Samuel out. Samuel started crossing the street rather than cross in front of the cottage next door, certain the man would leap out and snatch him away one day.

"Just don't pay attention to him, Samuel," his mother said. "He's just a sad, angry man, and it has nothing to do with you."

She didn't know. The library books taught Samuel that parents were often oblivious to what was truly going on. Adults tended to see what was on the surface and missed the sideways places.

The sideways places were the most important things, Samuel knew.

They glimmered and beckoned and called. Things entered and did not return. Other things emerged.

Like the man.

The rain fell in steady, drenching sheets, the way it had been for twenty-five days, non-stop. It grew a little lighter at times and whipped up wind and trees in the middle of the night, but mostly, it was the same, straight down, a monochrome fall of wet.

Samuel didn't mind, except it made it harder to keep his books dry. And it obscured his view of the sideways places. He figured he should feel relieved by that, but he knew that not being able to see or hear whatever was there was worse than seeing and hearing. He could still *feel* something. He just had no idea what was there.

The man next door really had stepped out of the sideways places one day. That was the thing his mother didn't understand.

"Oh, he just moved his things in when we were gone that Saturday. Don't you remember? We went to see Spiderman, and out for ice cream after."

But Samuel had seen him. He had seen him slide through the shimmering air in his hunched black coat and slope-crowned, broad-brimmed black hat, with his skin as white as moonlight on birch bark, and his chin and cheekbones sharp as knives. The man didn't have much nose to speak of, and it was hard to see his eyes.

Samuel felt the man stare at him that day. It was the last sunny day before the rains hunkered down in earnest that year. The last day of Autumn before the Winter came.

The man paused, the top of his face shaded into darkness by the hat, the white lower half of his face gleaming, and looked –Samuel was sure of it!– straight into Samuel's eyes. Then the man scuttled around the back side of the house next door.

There was no moving truck. No car full of boxes. Just a man who stepped out from a narrow slit in the shadows into the sun.

Things were okay for the first year or so. The man scuttled out now and then, but mostly stayed in the hulking cottage that used to be cute, with neat little curtains and a tidy stoop. But month after month, the house took on a more gloomy cast, even at the height of summer.

Then the rains returned.

And the neighborhood cats began to disappear.

At first, no one noticed. They figured the cats were hunkering down under houses or deep in the bushes somewhere, waiting for a break in the downpour.

The break in the rain never came. And neither did the cats. They insisted on going out, morning, noon, or night. And they simply failed to return.

Their humans stood, holding offerings of tuna and kibble, on broad porches and back stoops, and called the cat's use-names off the balconies of the apartment complex on the corner. The shouted names and rattling of food boxes disappeared beneath the steady sound of falling water.

And Samuel Lee? Samuel played cards with his Oma, did his homework, played online video games with his best friend Hal, and went to school. He tried to not pay attention to the rapidly crumbling cottage next-door, to the winds that whipped the tree branches and rattled his windowpanes every night. He tried to ignore the steady drenching rain.

But most of all, Samuel tried to pay no attention to the man next door.

Oh, he still saw him. Samuel saw the man all the time now. Out of the corner of his eyes, the man was waiting. When Samuel stepped off the school bus in the afternoons, he saw the shadow of the man's hat and the rain that bounced off the brim. But when he turned to look, all he would see was a mailbox, or a tree stump, or sometimes nothing at all.

Who would save Samuel Lee? The story was at a standstill. All he knew was that he was in danger.

Spiny hands grabbed at his arms. Spiny fingers turned his face. The fingers were like claws, like knives. Samuel lashed out with elbows and the heels of his winter boots. He struggled against his raincoat, tried to slip his arms out of the backpack that felt like it weighed 1000 pounds. Rainwater sluiced down his face, into his ears, his mouth, even up his nose. Samuel gasped and sputtered and fought and flailed.

"Get off me!" Samuel couldn't see what had attached itself to him, but if he had to place any bets, he would bet it was the man. "Let me go!" Samuel kicked out again, this time connecting with a shin. The spiny hands didn't lose their grip, not for one second. Samuel's mind raced, trying to remember what he learned from the three months of kid's judo his mother had forced him to take the year before.

He went limp, and all the fight dropped from his body at once. Startled, the hands let go.

Samuel ran.

He ran all the way toward the tan brick bulk of the library, where he was supposed to meet Hal and work on their history assignment. Dragging open the heavy wooden glass doors he flung himself into the shadowed vestibule, and stood panting, dripping water on the gray mat covering the marble floor. He peered through one of the panes of glass, but all he could see were the bare maple branches, waving in the wind, some cars, and the steady rain.

Samuel swept the hood off his head, wiped his face, and entered the library.

The library had been one of his favorite places since he was small. He loved the smell of books, the quiet murmuring of the librarians, and the possibility that he just might find the answers he was looking for. He might even find out the answer to the question who would save Samuel Lee. But he was starting to doubt that. Especially now.

The rows of metal shelving filled with plastic wrapped spines of hardbacks made way to paperbacks, and finally, to the wooden study carrels. He could see the top of Hal's spiky blond hair already bent over some books. Hal was as much of a nerd as Samuel was.

Samuel quickened his pace until he was standing right next to Hal. He slung his backpack off, and dropped it like a weight to the floor. Then he shook himself out of his raincoat and draped it over the back of a wooden chair.

"Dude, you're soaked." Hal was always one to state the obvious. "You okay?"

Samuel dropped into his chair and leaned in close, lowering his voice, "I think that man tried to grab me."

"For real? The weird guy? What makes you think it was him? What happened?"

Samuel explained as best he could, but it sounded strange even to his ears. Hal looked interested, because nothing weird ever happened to him, but Samuel could tell he was skeptical. Skeptical. That was their word of the week.

"Maybe it was nothing. I don't know. But something grabbed me, that's for sure."

"Should we tell somebody?" Howell said. "Like the librarian? Maybe other kids are in danger."

Samuel thought about it for a moment, then shook his head. Who was there to tell?

He woke in the darkness. For once, the wind didn't lash the windows, and the rain had receded to a steady patter.

The man was in his room. Samuel could feel him. There was a disturbance in the air, the kind that let you know you weren't alone. And if he tried, he could hear someone breathing under the sound of the rain. Samuel lay very still. He tried to think of what to do. Should he yell? Call his parents?

That didn't seem right. Samuel didn't know how he knew it, he just did. The man was mysterious, and maybe he made the cats disappear, but Samuel hadn't heard any stories of children disappearing.

He made his decision. Quick as lightning, he reached out for his Buzz Aldrin lamp and flicked it on.

The man peered out from underneath his broad-brimmed hat, his eyes still in shadow, his cheekbones like knives.

"What do you want?" Samuel whispered.

The man cleared his throat. It sounded like rocks tumbling down the hills onto the highway. It was strange. Samuel realized he didn't feel afraid anymore. The old man wasn't exactly a friendly neighbor, and maybe he was still some freak from the sideways worlds, but he was also just someone who happened to be sitting in Samuel's bedroom in the middle of the night.

Yeah... Maybe it was a little weird. Maybe Samuel was a little bit weird.

"She thinks you're ready." The man's voice carried all the weight of winter. It was filled with long, dark nights, the feeling of ice on the back of your neck, and the taste of rain.

"Who? Who thinks I'm ready?"

The man shook his head, just slightly, enough to shake the edges of the brim of that dark hat.

"If you're willing, put on your shoes and come with me." The man stood, coat pooling around his ankles, white fingers emerging from the cuffs, face still half-shadowed.

Guess it's up to you now, Samuel Lee, Samuel thought. He flipped back his Crab Nebula comforter and swung his feet to the cold floor.

S amuel carried his shoes down the stairs, pausing in the kitchen to slip them on and lace them. His coat hung on a hook near the back door. The air in the kitchen was cold and smelled like spaghetti sauce. He was glad he'd pulled a sweatshirt on over his pajamas. Buttoning the coat up all the way, he stepped outside. It was dark. But the rain was letting up, which was good. Samuel didn't feel like getting soaked again. He'd had enough of that lately. Everyone complained about the rain, and not just the usual complaints, because it rained every winter. But not like this, the people said. Not like the last three years.

Not like since the man moved in.

"This way," the man said. Samuel followed him into the dark of the garden towards the back gate. The gate swung open quietly on its well-oiled hinges. Something skittered through the bushes. Opossum, Samuel figured. A yellow streetlamp marked the space between Samuel's parents' home and the man's cottage. The man slid around the pool of light, and it set the edges of his hat and coat gleaming. Samuel wondered why he didn't walk straight through, but he figured better follow whatever it was the man was doing.

That was what the stories always told you. When someone came from a place that wasn't earth, you either ran as fast as you could, or you did exactly what they did. Because you never knew what misstep might end up trapping you.

You never knew what thing you ate or drank or said meant that you'd never see your family and home again.

They walked behind the cottage, and Samuel stifled a gasp. While the cottage was falling down, the garden had flourished.

Secret hollows were covered in ivy. Japanese Maples brooded over stones. From a back corner, Samuel caught the slight trickling sound of a waterfall. And, in the center of it all, circling row after row of blooming roses.

Samuel moved toward them, sniffing their perfume. Then he saw that the bushes weren't quite right. Some of the bushes were in full bloom, others were tipped with delicate buds, and interspersed between them all were the bare rosebushes of winter, fat rosehips gleaming red in the mottled light and dark.

"What is this place?"

There was no answer, so Samuel just followed the man, who seemed to be leading him directly towards the center of the rosebush circles. Samuel understood now why the cottage was so neglected; all the man's attention must've gone back here.

There was an opening between one bush filled with deep red roses, and another of the winter bushes whose rose hips were bigger than any Samuel had ever seen.

His Oma put rosehips into honey and ate them all winter long. Samuel liked the combination of tart and sweet. Mama said it was the best way to get vitamin C.

Oma was never sick, so they both must be right.

"Where are you taking me?"

The man just flicked his spiny knife fingers forward. Samuel followed.

And there she was. He could swear she hadn't been there seconds before, but she was there now.

Surrounded by roses, hair pale as moonlight tumbled down her shoulders until it almost reached the ground. The ground that was covered with maple leaves, oak leaves, ginkgo leaves, and the petals of pink and yellow roses. The man bowed deeply, sweeping the broad-brimmed hat off his head for just a moment. Samuel could see he was bald. And then the man stood tall again, hat back on his head, face in shadow. Leaving Samuel to stand and stare.

Her face was all flat planes and hollows, her skin the color of the walnut dresser in his Oma's room. Three birch trees shook their silvery leaves, their bark as pale as her hair. Like the old man's skin.

"Who are you?" Samuel asked the question, but he knew. He knew exactly who she was. And the man? He must be some sort of messenger or something. Kings and queens always had messengers, didn't they?

She spoke. Her voice sounded the way Samuel imagined a glacier cracking would sound.

"I am the Queen of Winter," she said. "And I have been waiting for you."

It didn't explain the cats. Later that night, back in bed, that was the thought that flickered through Samuel's mind.

What happened to the cats?

The hems of his pajamas were damp around his feet. He shivered beneath the Crab Nebula comforter and burrowed more deeply into his flannel pillow. Out of all the things he wondered, maybe that was a little strange, but Samuel wanted to know. He had a hard time falling asleep that night, but he finally did.

She should have been terrifying, but she wasn't. Instead, Samuel found himself wishing that instead of a rose garden at night they were sitting in front of the fireplace in his favorite rocking chair, the one so big he could sit cross-legged in it, a book propped on his lap. He would offer her the special hot chocolate his father made, the one with spices in it. She would like it, he was sure.

Instead, he stood shivering in the winter garden staring at the flat planes of her face, wondering why she called him there.

"I need the ones who see what isn't there," she said. "We always watch for the ones who pay attention. You've been seeing us for years, haven't you?"

Samuel froze in place, pinned like a beetle on a board. She was right. When he was five, he tried to tell his mother about it. She'd ruffled his hair and complemented his imagination. "But I'm not..." She smiled and told him to draw a picture.

So he did. He had notebooks filled with pictures that he would share only with Hal. Together, they made up stories about the sideways worlds and the people who lived there.

But he never thought to see one like this. Standing directly in front of him, with a voice like a glacier, and hair like the moon.

"I was never sure it was real," he said. "I mean, I only ever caught glimpses, you know?"

She nodded gravely. "That was by design."

Samuel shuffled his feet a little. His toes were getting cold. He cleared his throat. "So, um, the man, he said..."

"That I was waiting for you."

"Yeah."

"Follow me."

Samuel didn't remember what happened after that. All he knew was that the man was carrying him up the stairs to his bedroom. The spiny white fingers helped him off with his boots and tucked him into bed, leaving Samuel awake with his thoughts.

Night after night it happened. The man would wake him up, or sometimes Samuel would be reading, and the man would come. Samuel had learned to dress more warmly for bed. Sometimes it was raining now, sometimes not. And then the snow came.

The garden was white with it. Hushed with it.

Except for the ring of roses. The ring of roses looked as it had before. And there she was, with her moonlight hair and her walnut face arms crossed over her velvet chest.

"Are you ready this time?"

Samuel knew exactly what she was talking about. He nodded. "I want to go," he said.

And that was the truth; he *did* want to go. It had just taken him a while to work up to it. He finally figured out what had happened that first night. He had fainted. That was embarrassing, but oh well. The only thing that bugged him now about the situation was the fact that he hadn't told Hal. He just couldn't quite figure out how to talk to his best friend about it. Out of all the freaky stuff they discussed, this was a little too freaky.

But Hal would be pissed off that he hadn't invited him along. Maybe next time. After reconnaissance.

After Samuel had figured out exactly where this was leading.

He didn't see the doorway, the gateway, the whatever-it-was. One minute they were in the middle of the roses with snow sprinkling the garden all around them, and the next thing they were in a brick hallway —a corridor, the fantasy books called it. Torchlight sputtered and flared, lighting up the stones. Like, *real* torchlight. Iron rings bolted into the walls with flaming sticks thrust into them.

"Cool," Samuel whispered. He followed the long trailing velvet skirts of the Winter Queen. He could feel the man in the broad-brimmed hat behind. Samuel didn't know if that should make him feel safe or afraid. He shrugged. Might as well just go with it.

The hallway opened onto a vast hall with tall, vaulted ceilings held up by carved wood beams. There was an itching at the back of Samuel's eyes. He started to tear up. Then he sneezed.

Looking down at the flagstone floor he finally figured out where the cats had gone. There they were, dozens and dozens of them. Big orange bruisers, mottled tabbies, Siamese, even a Persian or two. They lapped at dishes of cream, reclined on fluffy cushions, or played with endless balls of red and yellow yarn.

Samuel laughed and laughed and laughed. The room was so huge his voice felt swallowed up. When he looked at the woman, she had a smile on her face.

"And that is why we called you here today. Our hob is sick. We need someone to care for all these cats."

"I don't get it," Hal said. "Why would the Queen of Winter need you to take care of the neighborhood cats? And why'd the cats run away in the first place?"

The boys were in Samuel's room, supposedly working on a science-art project. Popsicle sticks, glue, and construction paper littered the floor. The room smelled like the hot chocolate Samuel's dad had delivered half an hour ago. Samuel peered into his white mug. Yep. All gone.

"I'm not really sure. Not yet. None of it makes sense to me, though Strickleton says it 'will all be clear in time.' As if."

"Strickleton's the creepy guy next door? Why doesn't *he* take care of the cats?"

"I asked him that," Samuel replied.

S tricketon sniffed, a sniff that seemed too mighty to come from his tiny nose. His rocks-rolling-down-the-hill voice rumbled, "I," he said, "am the Gardener."

Just like that. Capital letter and everything. Gardeners, it turned out, did not take care of cats. Everyone in Sideways had a job and wasn't allowed to do anyone else's. And yeah, the hob who held the title of Cat-Herder was sick.

"You are perfect," the Winter Queen said. "We always offer gifts to the observant children like yourself. You shall grow up blessed, touched by our realms."

She'd paused then, and tilted her head his way. "Do you have a longing to be a poet?" she asked. "A bard? A painter, perhaps?"

"I want to be an astronomer!" Samuel blurted out.

The Winter Queen looked a bit disappointed at that. "Ah. I see. Well, the stars are nice, I suppose. We have different constellations here," she said. "We shall show them to you next time you come." The queen paused then, to drink deeply from a pretty golden cup. "If, that is, you agree to care for the cats for four phases of the moon."

Samuel rubbed at his eyes. He would really like

to see the Sideways constellations. But there was the one problem...

"I'm allergic."

"So you have to help me!" he said to Hal. "You love cats, right? And didn't Moggie run away last year? I bet she's there! You could find her again. Bring her home!"

Hal didn't look too keen about the prospect.

"I don't know Samuel, you sound kind of crazy, you know?" Hal was gluing popsicle sticks together, trying to form a geodesic dome. "We're not little kids anymore."

Samuel paced the carpet in his small bedroom, from bed to desk, to the door. He skirted around Hal, waving his arms with excitement.

"Don't you see? All those books we've read, all the stories..." Samuel stopped and flopped back down on the floor. He leaned toward his friend, whose blonde hair was even more spiky than usual. Samuel wondered if Hal had accidentally-on-purpose rubbed some glue into his hair. "What if they're true?"

Hal sat down two triangles on a piece of news-paper to dry. "I don't know, Samuel. I have enough trouble getting my parents to let me come over to your house. You really think they're going to let me traipse off to wherever it is?"

"But that's the beauty of it," Samuel said. "They won't know."

S ure enough, Samuel convinced Hal to join him. Samuel figured if he brought someone to take care of the cats—though he still wasn't sure why exactly the cats had gone to the sideways world— then maybe, just maybe, as a reward, the Queen of Winter would let them both see the stars.

"Holy shit," Hal said.

"I know, right?" Samuel looked around the hall, still impressed by the vaulted ceiling, the crisscross of wooden beams, and all the cats.

He turned to the man in the slouch-brimmed hat. "Do we wait here?"

The man started to walk, threading a pathway through the cats. His bone white lifelike fingers gestured them forward. Hal looked at Samuel. Samuel just shrugged and loped after the man's dark coat.

Hal tugged at Samuel's coat sleeve. "This is like some Dungeons & Dragons stuff," he whispered. Samuel nodded again and kept moving. He just hoped this deal was going to work.

They entered a brick hallway lit with the same

sconces, flames casting red and gold shadows every-where. It was strangely medieval. Samuel wondered if all the sideways worlds were like this, or if it was just this one in particular. Maybe the Queen of Winter just liked it this way. He wondered if the torches were magical, or if there was a Torch-Lighting-Hob that took care of them.

Just as suddenly as the corridor began, it ended, this time opening into a smaller room. The ceilings were just as high, but the walls were close in, forming a cozy space. Fire crackled in an enormous hearth which was flanked by two wolfhounds who twitched their ears and slit opened their eyes. Checking for danger? The dog on the left sighed and closed its eyes again. The dog on the right stretched and yawned, then trotted over to a large comfortable chair where the Queen of Winter sat, reading a book. Samuel would've expected a big tome with gilded edges, but it looked like an ordinary paper book from home. In her other hand, she held a half-eaten apple. The dog sat at her feet and whined. She looked up.

"Ah," she said, "I see you brought a friend to meet me." She held up the book. It looked familiar. "Do you like A Wrinkle in Time?"

It was one of Samuel's favorite books. "I love it."

The dark planes of the Winter Queen's face arranged themselves into what Samuel supposed was a smile. "Then I'm sure will be great friends."

She turned her eyes on Hal, who stood frozen to the spot.

"Are you the new Cat-Herder? You don't look like a hob. You look like a boy," she said.

Hal blushed, all the way from his T-shirt to his spiky blond hair. "Uhhh... Yes, ma'am. I'm just..."

The Queen tilted her head in question. Then she clapped her hands, "I know! You are a Bard! I can see it all around you. You must also be a friend of the Wind."

Samuel's jaw dropped. He stared at his friend, who only grew redder in the face. Hal sketched a shallow bow, then straightened up again.

"At your service, my Queen."

Wow. This sure was getting interesting, Samuel thought.

"How delightful," the Winter Queen said. "An Astronomer and a Bard." She turned to the man in the hat. "Well done, Strickleton. But what are we to do with all these cats?"

Strickleton moved forward, just as Hal burst out, "I'll take care of them!" Strickleton stopped in his tracks.

"Well, well, well," the Winter Queen said, "a Bard and a Cat-Herder combined. This is turning out better than I ever imagined. Would anyone care for some tea?"

And so the adventure began. Every evening between homework and bed, for four cycles of the moon, Hal would whistle at Samuel's window and off the boys would sneak to the hollow of roses in Strickleton's garden. Samuel studied of the constellations in the sideways realm while Hal brushed five cats a night in turn. The cat-herding hob did not return, so the boys continued.

After six months or six days or six years of this, the Queen of Winter rewarded Samuel with the most clever and cunning telescope and astrolabe he'd ever seen. For Hal, she procured a lute.

The cats, it turned out, liked the cream from the Sideways world better than the cream at home. Plus, there was always a soft cushion or a warm hearth to be had.

Mostly? The cats hated the rain.

And so the boys grew up together, making music and gazing at stars. Years later Hal became both a rock musician and a poet of some renown. He raised Maine Coon Cats in his spare time when he wasn't recording or on tour.

And Samuel Lee? It turned out he didn't need saving at all. He fell in love nine times, helped to raise three children, and mapped areas of space no one even knew existed before.

He also wrote illustrated children's books. The title of his most beloved work was *The Stars of Neverwhere*.

It's still in print today.

3

MURDER IN THE GARDEN

T he crime scene was clear.

There were signs of struggle on the front porch. The small rug, crumpled and disheveled, rested three feet from its starting point, and feathers were everywhere. And I mean everywhere. They coated the creased rug and lay in small drifts across the porch.

A sparrow carcass lay near the door, claws up in the rictus of death. It seemed like a small bird to have given up so many feathers.

Internally, I had named the neighbor cat "Murder-Bot" months ago, as I repeatedly interrupted it stalking the tall dried grasses in our backyard. It always looked annoyed when I did that. But truthfully? The handsome cat, with dark, seal colored tabby stripes, *always* looked annoyed. It was a cat that only suffered human existence in exchange for occasional shelter, and promises of food and water.

That cat lived its own life.

This morning, the name proved to be accurate. The cat is, indeed, a murderous beauty. And, despite whatever name my neighbor calls it —or me, for that matter— it stalks the yards under its own authority. Its own name.

As long as there are songbirds, Murder-bot knows its purpose.

Sighing, I left aside all thoughts of coffee, shucked my slippers and shoved my feet into boots. Then I clomped outside to get the shovel. The poor sparrow wouldn't take care of itself, but the soldier fly larvae in the compost heap would be happy to eat it into nothingness.

Coffee would wait until after I'd taken care of Murder-bot's handiwork.

H unting is joy. Blood on claw and tooth. The crunch of tiny bones. The sense of power.

But mostly, the focus. Stillness. Waiting. Stalking. Waiting. Collecting speed in muscles until...strike. Snap! Victory.

Even the occasional misses satisfy. They teach me other things I need to know. The arc of the trajectory. The inaccuracies in gauging speed.

All of these are fixable, with time.

I t was one week after the sparrow murder, and I was out back shoveling mulch, spreading it around the garden beds. I hoped to get one last round of autumn vegetables in before putting the garden to sleep for the winter.

There was a shining glimmer over by the small concrete bird pond I'd set into the ground beneath the persimmon tree. I had installed it, hoping to keep a garter snake around, but other than one sighting two springs ago, I hadn't seen the slender visitor again. No matter. The small birds loved the bath, as did the crows. And a raccoon family made use of it at night. So, I imagine, did the local opossums.

This looked like none of those, and it was far too late for butterflies. A downed hummingbird, perhaps? It had that sheen about it.

I knocked the mulch from the shovel and propped it against the garage, tugging my elbow-length work gloves off as I walked toward the cement pond.

"What the...?"

Hunting the Bright Things is harder. They fly or scurry in patterns I don't know.

But sometimes I catch one, all the same.

Resting against the curve of the half-empty cement bowl, was a tiny figure. It looked like the largest dragonfly I'd ever seen. Two of its wings were crumpled. But it wasn't a dragonfly.

I didn't know what it was.

That's a lie.

I *did* know what it was. I'd just never seen one before. And I didn't think they were real.

It had golden skin. And humanoid limbs with strange, attenuated, little hands. Huge eyes like those creepy paintings. Even clouded with death, I could see that once upon a time they were violet colored. It was the size of a robin or a jay.

It was a faery.

My mouth set itself in a grim line, and I shook my head. Then I spoke out loud to the garden:

"OK, Murder-Bot. Enough is enough.

The human was in my territory again, going about its business, disturbing the birds and mice.

I had a good spot in a bush near the fence. The earth was comfortable. Still warm enough, too. Twitching my tail, once, twice, thrice, I settled in to wait.

Sitting in my clean but crusty old kitchen that desperately needed updating, I brewed a pot of tea. Mint and lavender from the garden.

Carrying the white ceramic pot to the well-oiled wood table that served as a kitchen island and break-fast table, both, I groaned and eased myself into one of the ladder-back chairs. Gardening kept me fit, but shoveling mulch still made me feel my age.

I dragged my electronic tablet and stylus pencil

across the table and opened a notebook app. Though it already smelled delicious, the tea would take a few minutes to steep.

May as well get to thinking, Alyssa.

What did I know? The cat was a class A hunter. A murderer par excellence.

I wrote *"Cat is a killer"* in looping cursive script on the tablet.

"Seems to hate everyone" I wrote next. That seemed like a non-essential point, except that it was important to the nascent plan cooking in my head.

Pausing for a moment, I poured some tea into the delicate flowered cup I'd picked up as part of a mismatched set at my local charity shop. The herbs could still use more time to steep, but the pale greenish yellow brew would do for now.

Except, in order to write the next part, I needed more fortification.

Shoving back up from the table, I went to get the shortbread biscuits I half-hid from myself in the back of the cupboard. There should still be an unopened packet of the buttery treats.

The birds stayed in the higher branches. I would need to come back in the morning to catch the wrens and finches that foraged for pine seeds on the ground.

Besides, the sun was dimming. My human would be putting out some moist treats. Not as good as a mouse or bird, but they would do.

Still chewing the rectangle of butter and sugar held together with a modicum of wheat, I picked up the stylus and tapped at my lips. Was I thinking? Or was I avoiding writing the next damn thing?

Avoiding, definitely.

I forced myself to write the words. *"Faeries are real."*

I exhaled, and reached for the white porcelain pot again, pouring out more tea. The greenish yellow was darker this time, and even more fragrant. The scent should calm me. At least, that was the idea. But the way this was going, I would need a tot of whiskey by the time this list making was through.

Seriously, Alyssa? Faeries are real? I thought. But they were.

The proof was in a small box I'd lined with fallen leaves and mulch, then taped shut. I hadn't been able to bear throwing the creature into the compost, stupidly sentimental as that was.

All of my childhood books and dreams lay stiff and cold in a box on my back porch, and the murderous cat was still on the loose.

"What to do?" I wrote, followed quickly by, *"A: somehow contact the Faery Court or whatever."* As if I had a chance of that. What was I going to do, text them? Turn widdershins in my backyard under the full moon?

"B: Bell Murder-Bot."

So round. So plump. So small. So tasty.

I could almost hear the little bones snapping between my teeth as I sat beneath my favored bush, tail twitching in anticipation.

They were not snapping yet, but all good things came with time.

The round little birds took flight. Damn it! That lumbering human!

Large paw gripping my neck! I hissed. Yowled. Lashed out with my strong legs and razor claws.

"Damn it!" Murder-Bot had turned into a spitting wildcat. My elbow length work gloves, denim jacket, and jeans saved me from the worst of the claws, but the thing was damn hard to keep a grip on.

And I'd forgotten to protect my face. A claw slashed my cheek open.

"Damn you again!" I shouted, struggling to wrap the old wool blanket around the hissing whirlwind and get the back legs secured.

Maybe I should have gotten backup for this operation. Too late now. This would be the only time Murder-Bot would let me sneak up on it.

There was as sudden whirring near my head. I jerked and almost dropped the cat. Clutching tightly, I ducked my head and barely missed getting swiped by those claws again.

The whirring was bright, glinting in the weak morning sun. Faeries?

Tiny, brightly winged bodies wove in and out between my arms and the slashing murder claws. Time to change strategy. I gripped the blanket encased lower legs and held the struggling cat as far from my torso as possible. The faeries grabbed the blanket edges with tiny hands and wrapped the spitting cat's front paws, then pulled a flap of wool over its head.

I snatched it close to secure the whole thing. The faeries swooped away just in time.

No! Yowl! No! What was this thing? This thing that smelled of large animals. I fought with all my might. Spitting. Clawing with all my strength.

Then darkness.

Strange whirring sounds.

It was them. The Bright Things.

"What was your plan?" A voice behind me, sounding quite amused, the scent of wood smoke and loam.

I turned slowly, clutching the still squirming killer-in-a-blanket, and gasped.

The creature was beautiful. Just taller than my own 5 foot eight. Hair the color of midnight, woven through with pale birch branches. Skin the particular shade of leaves turning into dark mulch. Some sort of garment dyed cranberry red.

Whether it was female or male, or something else entirely, I could not tell, though it carried itself like a queen. All I knew was that my heart pounded in my chest. My mouth was suddenly dry, and I really wanted to pee.

I also wanted to fade into the background. To stand so still, they wouldn't notice me.

"Too late," the faery said.

It can read my mind?

"Of course I can. So, what exactly was your plan?"

"My plan?"

The faery inclined its head toward the bundle in my arms. Hmm. The murder-bot had calmed down. Either it liked being wrapped in a blanket, or the big faery had the same effect on the cat, it had on me. The cat wanted to disappear.

"T-t-to bell the cat. So the birds and the…um… faeries? So the birds and faeries could hear it coming and get out of the way."

"A capital idea!" The faery clapped its hands and two of the small, winged creatures swooped in and landed on its shoulders. The larger faery turned to one and then the other, whispering something in a language I could not understand.

Then the small faeries disappeared as if they had just…winked out.

"We shall bring a special bell and collar. And this is much better than what I was going to do."

"Which was?" The words were out of my mouth before I could call them back.

"Snap its neck."

My neck is scratched half raw. The thing will not come off. Even my human tried after I snapped at its hands and cried, but no. The infernal tinkling starts up every time I move.

No more, the thrill of the hunt. No more, the juicy flesh. No more crunchy bones.

It is all dried up kernels in a bowl, and moist treats that do not satisfy.

My life is hell. My purpose is no more.

Winter settled in, and the steady rains and dark sky reign. There's a snap in the air that speaks of frost, and maybe even snow.

There are no more crime scenes on the front porch. No more carcasses for the compost. The faeries took the body of the victim from my box and winked out of sight, carrying it with them.

The larger faery creature? Part of me wanted to know what it was. Part of me hopes I never see it again.

Murder-Bot glares at me from my neighbor's porch, or from the side window. It never comes into my yard anymore.

My house is in order and the gardens are at rest. Stew bubbles in the slow cooker, and the stove is gleaming and clean. My house is in order and the gardens are at rest. There is only one thing left to do.

With a smile on my face, I pull a sack out from the pantry. A bag of seeds for the finches and wrens.

4

———

THE BUOYANCY OF LIGHT

Zara yanked her keys from the lock and pushed the door open with her shoulder. Weighted down with a laptop case, her favorite bright red leather bag, and a sack of groceries, her arms and shoulders ached, and she just wanted to get inside. Inside to the blue painted apartment that was all her own.

"Holy shit Chastaine. Again?" Zara had learned to curse only in the last year, after finding she liked the way the words ran sharp against her teeth before exiting her mouth. She wrestled her variety of bags onto the breakfast bar that separated the pocket kitchen from the open living room of her one bedroom apartment.

She could smell Chastaine's excitement: that strange doggy smell of rides in cars and romps in grass. A mixture of warm sun on fur, excess saliva, and joy.

Rolling her aching shoulders, Zara turned toward the small grouping of deep blue couch, wooden coffee table inlaid with metal, and her favorite: the green velvet arm chair she'd found on the street and dragged up the two flights of stairs to be hers. Above the chair, her golden haired spaniel Chastaine floated five feet in the air, limbs splayed out, ears drifting sideways, and tail whacking at the air. Pure doggy bliss was on her face.

It was her sister, Rayma, trying to steal her dog. Zara just knew it. Her sister always cooed and ah'ed over the dog when Zara sent visions of her life back home, out past Alpha Centauri, to the green fields and golden waters of the Timoka province on Zulack.

She ruffled Chastaine's floating ears. They were so soft. Soft like the fluff from the peepo plants right before harvest. Soft like Hazik's baby cheeks. Soft like the taste of her father's hermet – that early harvest distillation of the green shoots that grew by the river, tasting of what humans here called honey, and spring.

Chastaine sighed, more relaxed and contented than Zara could ever recall being herself. She hadn't relaxed in the three years since her exile.

Really, the only thing better about being on earth was Chastaine. There were no dogs on Zulack. Not that she'd ever heard of. There were marvelous creatures on her home landmass alone: swimming endeelies, flying scorpanas, and the fierce taramors that ran the wild lands. Zara had seen visuals of other beasts in parts of Zulack she had never visited. That kind of roaming was best done when one was was old, in one's mid-hundreds, when one had worked enough to ensure that family would remain preserved and was still of vigor enough that one had years before entering the ancestor's halls. Zara would never see the places those beasts traversed. She would die here in this hard place, far from the soft light she loved.

They said she had betrayed her people and were going to give her the ochre pill that would solidify her blood and muscles, turning her from flesh to stone, until her hearts stopped beating in syncopation. One would stop first, signaling to the other organs to begin shutting down. Then the second heart would slow its beating, as she went slowly blind and deaf, as taste fled from her tongue, until finally, there would be nothing. Rock dust. Inert.

No chance to make the final offerings to her Gods, no pouring of wine for the ancestors, for she wouldn't be joining their ranks of honor. No opportunity for one last kiss before consciousness fled, just deep internal monitoring as first this system, and then that, shut down.

How did she know this? The biology of it had been described in detail by the judiciary scientist one day. Her particular province in the great land mass of Timoka believed in letting people know exactly what they were getting themselves into. They said that it was kinder that way, so there were no surprises. Zara wondered at that. It seemed rather that the information would be used to terrify, so the final moments were all suffused with fear. A little extra jolt of punishment for a being that would be beyond all punishment when the process was done.

Nobody knew what happened to the dishonorable dead. As children, they were taught that the souls would be torn apart and scattered to the fifty planets. Adults argued about it all, of course. Some held with those teachings, while others said the dishonorable dead had their own corner of the ancestral realms, forever in exile. Still others said the Gods all turned their faces, looking away, and the dishonorable dead were therefore not under rule of order and could wander, causing mischief in the least, and at the most, great pain, pestilence, even war.

It was these believers who kept the anti-conjuration shops in business: buying charms to ward off revenants and disease. Their homes were known by the woven rushes hung above their doors in season, and the soot that marked their lintels when the storm times brought the cold.

"In this age, such superstition should not have a grip on us!" her father used to rail. He was an advanced man. A rationalist who nonetheless wrote poetry. Zara's mother would nod and agree. Xenori had the most education of all in their families, holding ten degrees in the arts and in three sciences. Kendrik had wooed her with his steady mind and his lyric poems. They'd been together for one hundred years.

Zara would never know that kind of love.

But the close kin to that love had saved her life.

Chastaine's softness was cradled in her arms and the beam of light was gone. Zara's bones ached as always and there were tears on the still unfamiliar mounds of her cheeks. After the bargain had been struck – exile to earth instead of dissolution into stone – a different kind of dissolution process was begun, one that shifted her shape from seven prehensile limbs and a torso sheathed in rounded, russet skin, to this flat brown angular body with arms and legs that ached like nothing she else she knew. Funny, her body now was closer to Chastaine's shape than the one she lived with for thirty nine years. But the humans here saw dogs and cats and other four-limbed, headed and torso'd creatures as highly distinct. As lesser species than their own.

Chastaine just spoke differently. And worried less.

"Shit." She wiped at the moisture on her face. That word seemed ever appropriate here.

Zara sank into the green arm chair and gently rubbed her nose across Chastaine's fur. That scent of earth spring again. And warmth.

Despite the aching in her limbs, the isolation from those who knew her, the inability to meld with anyone her age – forty two on earth was more like eighty Zulackan, and twenty seemed a different kind of young than hers – Zara supposed it was still good to be alive.

There had always been friendly competition between the sibs, and Rayma was a little spoiled, but if Rayma knew the comfort Chastaine gave her, she would not try to steal the dog from this place. Zara kissed the top of Chastaine's head and rose, setting her onto the wooden slats of the floor. Chastaine's nails clicked companionably as she followed Zara toward the tiny kitchen to see what food was there.

"Zara!" The sound waves bent themselves through space and toward her ears.

Rick. That was the voice of Rick.

She'd learned to distinguish the subtle gradations of pitch and tone her first months here. Tones at home were more varied, but less cacophonous. Here, sounds seemed to crash together, so close to one another at first she thought four sounds were one. As she learned to regulate her one-hearted body with her breath, as she learned to work the hands and feet at the end of these four limbs, so she learned to tune her senses to this place.

Car engines and trucks in variance. Musical notes and tempos. Animals and birds. The way wind shooshed against the windows of home dwellings and whistled through the tall structures of downtown. The whir of bicycles, which terrified her. The different scent of water here. And different tastes, as well. Milk. Coffee. With Rick she had tried whisky.

Arranging some pleasantness on her face, she turned to face the tall man walking toward her. His hair was clipped short to his head. She knew the texture of it, barely giving way, moving past the whorled galaxies of her fingertips. His long stride carried him smoothly toward her. Rick walked as though the gravity of this place was of no consequence. As though his shins did not ache with it, and his heart did not labor to pump its blood.

Zara found his visage lovely. He was the color of sun on drying boka grain. She felt a stabbing in her belly as she always did when seeing him. Somehow, foreign though he was, Rick always sent her mind to home.

"How you doin' gorgeous?" That was his way. Easy. Familiar. Zara knew it was not just with her. She had seen him greet the bartender that way, when ordering their drinks in the dark place lit with jewel-like glass. She saw that he was friendly with the other females, too, but noticed he did not lean into them so close as he did her.

She was not sure yet what it meant, but found she liked the way he turned his eyes toward her.

"I am fine today, Rick. How is your week so far?"

"You know, I'm a working man."

Zara knew that she should tease him about being

a working man, for he wore a suit so fine the threads were barely visible. She knew by now that he had money, and what he did in the downtown towers was hardly toil. She still didn't quite trust what that teasing should look and sound like, so she kept quiet.

"What's happening in that mind of yours, sister?"

Sister. She wasn't sure why he called her that. Though it seemed to be a term of some esteem for him, it didn't mean what she had learned it to mean. Yet. Rick fell into step beside her, which confused her more. She hadn't been going anyplace in particular, but knew that this would be considered strange. He would expect her to have a destination. She didn't.

She was still getting her bearings in this city – a smaller place than the one she had first landed in, which had almost killed her with overbearing noise and confusion. This city had rounded trees, and giant puffballs of blue and purple flowers that she loved. Hydrangea. Her daily sojourns were educational. One could learn a lot if one simply wandered. Watched. Listened.

That was how they met. She had wandered into the giant repository of histories and fantastic tales filled with sorrow and learning and joy. The bright spines of the books were every color she had seen on earth so far, and even some that reminded her of home. The smell of dried and pressed plant matter was pleasing to her, as was the smell of the coffee and sugar she had learned to love. Turning the corner between Ancient Rome and Contemporary American History, her body had bumped into his own. They had both hurried to apologize, laughing, flustered.

He had bought her coffee and some sweet delicacy made of the ground flour of almond nuts and bark from the cinnamon tree. She learned so many things here, every day. Almost like a child.

The way Rick made her feel was not the way a child would feel.

He was in his 30s, which put them at a similar rate of aging, now that she was in the midst of earth atmosphere and gravity. Her forty two years made her feel so young sometimes, and her learning rate increased this sense. But he treated her with the friendly deference of one with equal status. "Shit."

He laughed. "You always surprise me when you come out with that. You usually speak so formal, but you seem to love that word."

She smiled back. "I didn't mean to say that just then. But it has a sharpness about it. It seems direct."

"Direct. Yes indeed."

They walked in silence past plate glass windows and spindly trees, cafes filled with baby-toting parents and people hunched over notebooks and computer tablets. A bicyclist whirred by, a flash of green and black. Zara contained her startlement.

Rick was turning toward her again. Zara looked up at his gold-brown face.

"I need to get off to a meeting, gorgeous, but I'm glad I ran into you. You never answer your cell."

She always forgot the small white com link that had been in the packet of earth things provided upon her release. Her father, snorting tears back from his orifices, explained to her how it worked, but she barely paid attention, focusing on the fact that she wouldn't see him again.

"What did you wish to ask me?"

"Will you have dinner with me tomorrow night?"

Zara paused, rubbing her hands across her aching elbows. Looked up at Rick's bright, expectant face. "Yes. I will."

She wandered through the city, wondering. What would they talk about, if time continued to hold them in its arms? What would she tell him?

After hours, her feet and hungry belly took her home.

Entering her blue apartment she saw Chastaine floating again.

But the beam of light was larger than before.

"Chastaine? Rayma?" She sniffed the air. Nothing different. Just the light and Chastaine's happy scent.

The beam shimmered through the green chair, rising toward the ceiling, then winked out. Chastaine dropped softly to the chair with a little whine, then stretched and turned her eyes to Zara.

"What is happening, Chastaine? What are we to do?"

Rayma was the beautiful one, all deep red skin that lay in gentle folds. Her limbs were always moving out in waves, expressive and grace filled. She was often laughing, but not on that day. The day of sentencing. That day, her limbs lay quietly around her body. Rayma's face was grave.

They were in the meeting place. Friezes of judges for the last ten thousand years lined the walls, all glimmering with minerals, reflecting the illumination in the room. The judge was perched on the Ancestor Seat, the padded throne that conferred the wisdom of the ages to the one prepared to sit there. He was the oldest person Zara had seen.

Her mother Xenori had hired a team of lawyers in order to present her case. They had gathered information, and spoken to all manner of beings and people. All Zara could do was shake her head and say nothing had happened. That she didn't know.

She hadn't even been there. The incendiary was not of her making. She had neither the knowledge nor the willingness.

(They had never meant the castle to catch fire.)

"Traitor to your caste," she had been called. It was likely true, though her parents had always taught her tolerance and ease with all the beings of Timoka. They had the ease of wealth, but always tried to be fair and kind.

(She hadn't known that day would be the day.)

Her visuals were everywhere, spread far throughout the province. She was famous for having been charged. For being alive. All her friends were dead.

If she was traitor to anything, she was a traitor to her cause.

(They hadn't told her about the meeting. She had thought they trusted her...but not enough.)

Zara lay awake on her soft bed, the only comfort for these strange joints and aching bones. Ankles. Knees. Elbows. Hips. Cradled into softness, they almost felt like hers. But she knew that hauling this oddly fashioned body about was the only way to keep it strong. She had been told that, by the scientist, before leaving her home.

She had also been told that the body needed more rest than her body on Zulak. That she was supposed to sleep. She did this in short cycles, until the pain in her limbs caused her to shift position, waking her again.

Chastaine was a weighty lump at the bottom of the bed, pinning down the blankets in deep sleep. Zara crept her way out, sliding feet into cushioned slippers that eased the small bones of her toes, and reminded her arches to hold the shapes of bows.

She released waste water in the bathing room without bothering to turn on the illumination switch.

The lawyers had done their job well. Zara remained alive, but the public still needed her punished, and her life was no longer really her own. Her life belonged to the histories now, and would be frozen in the memory of time. To continue her life as it had been would not be possible. The only thing left was sheer erasure. No more contact. No more memory. No more home.

Hence exile to this bone crushing planet, to build a life as best she could, away from Rayma and Xenori and Kendrik.

At least she had Chastaine.

Washing her hands, she turned to go back to bed. Noticed a glimmering. Walked toward the living room instead.

The beam of light was larger. Large enough to surround the velvet chair. Large enough to bathe the green in light so pure and strong the chair was glowing in the darkness.

Zara paused. Listened. No ticking of Chastaine's toenails on wood floor. Just the gentle hum of refrigeration and a distant sound of cars.

The light was silent.

"Rayma?" she whispered. She wasn't certain why, but she knew somehow this light was her sister's doing. Rayma always liked to tinker so.

Creeping toward the chair, she reached her right hand into the beam, fingertip by fingertip, then all the way down to her palm.

The light felt like weightlessness. Softer than her bed. Softer than Chastaine's fur. Yet it was textured. Textured like the coils of Rick's hair, or roughly woven fabric, soft yet *there.*

The bones in her right hand didn't hurt. She withdrew her hand quickly.

Walking around the chair, she climbed upon it, folding her limbs so they were contained within the beam.

She began to float.

The light held her. The light supported her. The light surrounded her body, pulling her aloft, weightless yet in stasis. Not touching the ceiling, yet hovering above her favorite chair.

For the first time in three years, Zara relaxed. The deep ache left her bones. The joints of this strange body ceased to throb.

She sighed.

"Thank you Rayma."

She could rest here. She slept, cradled in the softness of a sister's gift.

If she could rest, she could learn better. If she could rest, she might figure some things out. If she was freed – even so briefly – from the constant pain, she might be able to live. To figure out this city.

There was hope.

There was even a human called Rick. And a sweet, soft dog called Chastaine.

She had sent Rayma a message and finally got her answer back. This had taken most of three months. By this time she was seeing Rick once weekly. Zara had figured out that they could speak about what was in books, and that was enough. They could watch the primitive moving pictures on big screens in a crowd, or curled up on his couch at home. They talked about those, too. He had asked a question or two about her past, but seemed content for now that something terrible was in her history that she would not speak of yet. Offering small tidbits of his own, she felt that he was hopeful of her own revelations, but would wait longer.

Zara had some time.

Rayma told her that she had spent the years working on the beam, calibrating the equations just so, testing the weightlessness and the rate of transmission...and the cloaking of it all.

Zara was forever in her debt. She realized, one raining winter day, that she wanted to make offerings to the Gods. She gathered approximate ingredients: wine, grain, oil. She prayed for her sister's health, happiness, courage, strength, and well being. Zara continued this practice, refilling the cup and oil on the new and full phases of the moon that pointed her thoughts toward home.

She would find the Gods of this place, and see if they were the same. She started giving food out to the beggars, recalling how the Gods came in disguise.

The beam of light eased her every day. Over time, she felt that she was healing. That the gravity did not pull so hard and strong. She wasn't striding like Rick yet, but she felt better.

One morning she awakened to find the wine in the altar cup had been drunk down, and there was grain scattered in the oil.

Her gift had been accepted. Rayma would be blessed.

She was blessed, too.

After getting dressed, she wandered to the kitchen, following the sounds of Chastaine lapping water from her bowl.

"Shall we go for a walk today my friend?"

Chastaine wagged her tail.

THE DAY THE MAGIC FOX APPEARED

W hat a shitty day.

It was roasting hot outside. I was sweating, and my bike had gotten a flat tire en route home from work. And before that, I'd had to stop some stupid assholes from harassing the houseless guy that panhandled in front of the game store. People being jerks seemed to be on the rise.

Plus, I was hangry.

Ignoring my growling stomach, I pushed my way into the bathroom down the hall. The house felt empty. Housemates were all still at work. That was good. I could use a little quiet.

I splashed cold water on my face in the cracked white basin, and reached, for the bright orange towel.

It moved. I swore it did.

Don't be a doofus, Candy.

I grabbed the towel and mopped at my face then spluttered.

My lips were stuck with... fur?

"Gross! What the hell?"

I blinked, and scraped my hands across my face, trying to clear the disgusting whatever-it-was from my mouth and cheeks. Fur, like hair, sticks to wet things. I needed a towel. My towel.

"Sorry about that," said a small, raspy voice. "Poor timing on my part. But I really needed to talk to you."

My heart pounded and sweat broke out on the back of my neck. Whipping my head around, I scanned the room one-eyed, the other eye shut against what was likely one thin strand of fur but felt like a whole sweater.

I looked down, and leapt back, crashing into the shower door. "Ouch!"

There was a fox in the bathroom. A big fox. All orange and bristly, with black paws, a black nose, and a damn white tip on its bushy tail.

"What the hell?"

"You're repeating yourself, so I will, too. I apologize for my poor timing." The fox started speaking slowly, as if to a small child whom it really needed to understand. Its black tipped snout moved, though I had no idea how it was forming human words. "I... need... to... speak... with..."

"Oh, cut it out! I hear you. Just... go to the kitchen! I've got to wash my face again. If you've left me any clean towels!"

"Oh, that towel is quite clean, I assure you. Or as clean as it was when I arrived. You may wish to change it out though. It smells as if you've been using it for at least a week, and towels are bacteria breeding grounds..."

I pointed to the door. "Out."

The fox dipped its head, then trotted past me on dainty black feet. I shoved the door closed and looked down at the towel. No fur. I sniffed it. The fox was right. The towel needed changing. But I could deal with that later.

Hanging the towel back on the rack, I turned the

water back on and bent to wash my face. I used soap this time.

I opened the bathroom door and heard the soft rumble of the electric kettle and the clink of spoons. What the hell? Yeah. Maybe I needed a different phrase. But this whole situation was utterly surreal. Sure, a fox cleric was my go-to RPG character, but that didn't mean I expected an actual talking fox to have shown up and done something weird to my towel.

Or be able to work my kettle.

As I clopped my sneaker'd feet down the bright hallway, I tried to get my shit together. I entered the red and white decorated kitchen with the worn black and white linoleum tiles, and the clacking Felix-the-Cat wall clock. The fox had dragged a chair over to the crappy white countertop and was pulling a mug from the cupboard with its mouth. I about lost it.

"How the?" Great, Candy. Real articulate.

But really? All I had wanted was to get my limping bicycle home, wash my face, and stare out the living room with a cup of tea in hand. I was so not prepared for a face full of fur and a fox in my kitchen.

"You're pretty easily surprised for a person who spends so much time dreaming up ogres and wizards and going on whole adventures with them. Do you take milk in your tea?"

The fox looked at me with big dark eyes rimmed in white and black. For the first time I noticed, it was kind of beautiful.

Saying nothing, I walked to the 'fridge and pulled out a small carton of half-and-half.

"How are you gonna pour that?" I finally asked, jerking my chin toward the shiny red electric kettle.

"By using your hands," it replied, cool and calm as you please.

I set the carton down, got two tea bags from the glass canister on the countertop, and poured. The fox trotted over to the small red table tucked by the window that looked out onto our overgrown back-yard. Hopping up on one of the white wooden chairs, tail curled around its black paws, the fox sat straight-backed. Waiting for me.

"Do you take milk in your tea?" I asked. Two could play the cool-as-you-please game.

The fox tilted its long snout down. "Of course," it replied.

Of course a magic talking faery fox takes milk in its tea, I thought. What else would you expect?

I plunked the heavy mugs down on the table and sat down. Scrubbing my hands across my face, I released a sigh.

You'd think I would feel ecstatic to have a talking fox in my kitchen, but really? Sometimes a person just wants an ordinary life, you know? No matter how much we play at knights and castles, dragons and magic amulets, we actually just want a stable job that pays the bills and a place to sleep at night.

The fox sniffed at the steam curling out of the mug.

"So," I picked up my mug and took a sip. "What's your name? And are you going to explain what you're doing here? Also, my towel? Seriously? What kind of magical creature uses a towel as a portal, for Gods' sakes?"

The fox lapped at the tea, long tongue flicking out delicately, rolling the liquid into its mouth.

"My name is Tracy," it said. "And why not a towel?"

"I thought you..." I waved a hand in the air, "types."

The fox arched one bushy eyebrow.

"You know, faeries, magical beings, whatever," I continued. "I thought you used mirrors as portals."

The fox sighed and lapped up more tea. I was amazed that it could drink from a mug and not spill anything. I could barely manage that some days.

"Different beings use different things. I like towels. They're soft and easy to manage. Mirrors are hard and cold and feel weird when you're halfway through. Walking through a towel is like walking through a sunbeam. Besides, what makes you so sure I'm a magical being?"

I shook my head.

"That towel thing is bizarre, but okay. And why do I think you're magic? Come on. You use towels as inter-dimensional portals, and you talk. Plus..." I paused and gave the animal another look. "You kind of glow around the edges."

The fox didn't reply. I took that as a yes, I'm magical but not admitting it, answer.

"Not being a magical fox myself," I said, "I'll take your word for the portal thing. And I hope you give me some credit here for not being a gibbering mess on the floor right now. Most people would be, you know."

I could swear the fox smiled.

"That's why I'm here," it said. "You're not most people."

Now, everyone wants to hear they're special, but color me skeptical. Telling someone "you're not like other fill-in-the-group" is the oldest con in the book.

It was my turn to raise an eyebrow. So I did, and drank more tea. A hummingbird buzzed the window. The fox jerked its head toward the glass and gave that snout-dipping nod again. The hummer buzzed away.

Okay. Were all the local creatures in on this?

"What I mean," the fox continued, "is that you have a unique confluence of an open and curious mind, a flexible sense of reality, no family you're responsible for, and you already have skills in the area I'm interested in pursuing."

"And what area is that?"

"You understand fantasy role-playing games."

"You want us to what?" Rina yelped. We were hanging out in the living room, arrayed on the cozy overstuffed couch, feet up on the battered coffee table. Rina, a short, curvy, brown-skinned creampuff of badass, tapped the toes of her boots together in irritation.

"Yeah," said Solomon, lighting up a joint. "I don't get this at all."

A big, pasty, Jewish dude with five o'clock shadow and a black leather kippah, he sat on one of the matching club chairs covered in fake-tapestry-blankets with stylized dragons on them. What can I say? We're geeks, and we're relatively broke. He passed the joint my way. I handed it to Rina.

Things were weird enough as it was. I needed as clear a head as possible to explain the entity hiding out in my bedroom.

Tracy.

A talking fox.

"I'll need you to suspend disbelief for a minute. Pretend you're in a new RPG, okay?"

Rina huffed and crossed her arms over her ample chest. Solomon took another puff on the joint and nodded before tapping it out in an ashtray. He was a two puff a day guy.

"A magic fox came to us with a proposition."

"To us?" Rina asked. Maybe she needed more pot. That one puff hadn't made her any more chill, that's for sure.

"Yes. Well, to me, first. But it can use our help."

"And what is it that this fox wants us to do?" Solomon asked.

"It needs humans to collaborate on a game. To seed more magic in the world, it said." I was kind of wishing I'd taken a hit off the joint now. Rubbing my hands on my jeans, I took a breath. "It says the realm of faery is in danger of completely separating from the human world if more humans don't start to believe."

Solomon leaned forward, elbows on the knees of his black cargo pants. "Seems like that would be a good thing for faery," he said. "Less interference by human bullshit. Just let us go our way. Make our own mistakes. Orchestrate our own demise."

"Well, that's cheerful," Rina said. She touched my arm. "I still don't get it, though, Candy. Are you making shit up? Or is this fox real? Like physically real? Or what?"

I angled my head and called up the stairs.

"Tracy! We're ready for you!"

Well, that was an overstatement, wasn't it? No one could be ready for a talking fox.

Tracy's slender orange form appeared at the top of the oak staircase.

"You called me?" Their raspy voice was quiet, barely audible over Solomon's heavy breathing and the strange, mewling noise Rina was making with her throat.

"Yes. It seemed simpler to introduce you in person. Come down?"

Tracy barely made a sound on the creaky old stairs, disappearing behind the couch for a moment, before emerging into the living room.

"Holy shit," Solomon breathed out. "You're an actual, talking fox. Just like in the games."

Tracy leapt up onto the other chair, circling three times before settling onto the second dragon fake-tapestry-blanket.

"What do you want to know?" the fox asked.

Rina and Solomon looked at each other. Then at me.

They both avoided looking at the fox.

"Go ahead," I finally said. "What do you want to ask?"

Rina swallowed, hard. She was trembling a little. I stopped myself from reaching out to grab her hand. I had a feeling this was something she had to do herself.

"So…" her voice was reedy, as if she wasn't getting enough air. Rina cleared her throat and tried again. "Candy says you need help. That faery will separate from the world or something?"

"That's right," Tracy replied.

"And why isn't that a good thing?" Solomon asked, running a hand over his stubble.

The fox fixed him with its dark gaze. Solomon stared right back. I was impressed. He seemed to be recovering quickly, though I could see his fingers tapping, likely wanting to light up the joint again.

"If the realms separate completely, one of the worlds will die."

The words hung in the air like smoke from a California wildfire.

"And it won't be faery, will it?" Rina asked.

Tracy gave a little shrug of its small, umber shoulders. "Could go either way. But the way humans are going so far? It's likely that your realm will be the one to die. Or at least your race."

"Like, the human race?" Solomon rumbled.

"Exactly," Tracy replied.

Solomon and Rina both looked at me again, waiting for me to say something. To be the Dungeon Master in charge of this new game.

"If you're in," I said, "we should order up a pizza and make a plan."

Solomon slipped his cell from one of the many pockets on his cargo pants and hit dial. He had at least three pizza places programmed into his phone.

"One meat, one veggie okay?"

"Extra cheese, please," the fox said.

"You eat pizza?" I asked.

"Doesn't everyone?" it replied.

That was five years ago.

Slowly, the story came out. Tracy had been watching me for a while, peering through curtain fabric and towels, making sure I was the right one. I didn't want to think about that too hard. If Tracy saw some things that were embarrassing, the fox kept it to itself.

I now have a pretty good job running a small gaming company, with Rina and Solomon as my seconds in command. Together, we've made enough to put a down payment on a house. Who wants to live alone? Our friends test drive the games, for the price of a pizza and snacks.

Tracy literally pops in once a week to confer.

What does Tracy get out of it? The fox insists

we're saving the world. Sometimes I still find that hard to believe.

But then again, we're still here, aren't we?

And anything that makes the world a little more fun and magical? That's okay by me.

THE LIBERATORS

R alph liked living in the lab just fine.

Oh, the smells were not that great. There was a sharp, astringent scent that filled the air at least once a day that he particularly did not care for. And the light was a bit harsh at times, bouncing off the white walls.

Ralph didn't like that.

But he liked the other kittens. The other kittens smelled warm. And soft. Like milk and naps.

He liked the Piles of Blankets, too. The Piles of Blankets came in pleasant colors and smelled like kittens.

And Ralph liked the food well enough. Once he was weaned, and onto soft, solid food, he was treated to a whole array of tastes and scents he did not even know were possible before.

So yes, the lab was fine.

Though he didn't care for getting poked and prodded much. He particularly did not like the probes attached to his skull once a day. They stung a bit at first, then itched, and made it hard to move. But he did like the pets and scratches he got and the treats for being such a good kitty after the tests were done.

But the thing Ralph liked most of all?

Flying.

He loved to scamper and run, and bounce. And he loved to leap. And then, one day, the leaping turn to flying. Amazing!

Now Ralph flew every single chance he got.

Ralph was a champion flyer, the white coats said. Best of his litter.

Now, if only he had opposable thumbs. Because he would like nothing more than to fly in the scrap of blue he could see through the high, bolted window up above.

A kitten could dream, couldn't he?

"There's a new litter in need of rescue," Bruiser said, stalking back-and-forth in front of her comrades. "They're weaned now, so just old enough to break free. The question is, how are we going to do it this time?"

A dozen cats sat in a loose semicircle on the cracked concrete floor of the cavernous space. The cats lived in a compound in an old human-made warehouse, with high, wooden walls, dark rafter beams, and the faint smell of oil and, of course, cat. Not urine, though. The older ones trained the new recruits to use the latrine areas well away from the shelter of the building.

No one peed on a blanket and lasted very long in the freehold. Kittens excepted, of course.

The crew gathered in front of Bruiser were the current core committee. The rest of the compound cats were out hunting, patrolling, or training up the latest litter.

Bruiser was a battered cat who had battled many a battle and fought many a fight. She was in her prime, and could take on any cat in the freehold. That was why she currently held leadership, though no position was permanent among the compound cats.

She stalked back and forth, tail held high to show her authority. But a cat didn't just take charge, not here. A cat was given the honor of leadership for as long as it served the rest of the freehold, or until the leader decided they'd had enough.

That was the way of things.

First of all, you never knew when disease or a predator would take a comrade down, and second, cats just didn't like to work under anyone's authority for long. Oh, trading expertise was well and good. And someone needed to be the final voice sometimes. But mostly? Cats were anarchists. They did their own thing, and if what you wanted to do was what they wanted, too? Well that was all right then wasn't it?

"How can we be sure these kittens want to go?" Celeste asked. Celeste was a small, attractive tabby cat. She was currently catting around with Tom, a handsome marmalade fellow that Bruiser had tumbled with a time or three in the recent past.

"We'll have to ask them, won't we?" said Bruiser. "After we tell them what is possible outside the confines of their cages."

"After we tell them they don't need to be *experimented* on," growled Tom.

"That's right," Pipsqueak, a small, black and white cat, piped up. "They have to be running the tests on them by now. No one likes the tests."

Pipsqueak shuddered, as if remembering.

They all remembered.

Every cat paused in silence for a moment. They all had their stories—of the lab, or of the streets. They all had the memories that hunted them at night.

"I say we break them out first, ask questions later." That was Hemingway, an older gray cat with handsome whiskers and six toes on each foot. He had trained himself to use those toes like humans used their hands. Hemingway was quite useful, and only spoke when it was necessary, so the rest of the cats tend to listen to him.

Bruiser stopped and scratched behind an ear, throwing up an arc of sparkles that meant her powers brewed close to the surface, ready to burst free. Bruiser's magic was far-seeing and teleportation of small objects, which came in handy in all sorts of situations.

"I agree with Hemingway," Celeste remarked. "If the kittens want to go back to the lab after we bust them out? Well, that's up to them."

Tortoise—a fighting cat with flying powers—cleared his throat. "We can explain to them what their options are once we have them here. We can't do that while they're locked inside."

"So what's the plan?" Pipsqueak asked.

"That's what we need to figure out," Bruiser replied.

There was always too much to figure out, even for uncommon cats like they were. They all had magic, extra powers, or unusual skills of one form or another. Some of them came by them naturally, and others were human implanted. But there was no hierarchy of talent here. They were all just cats, living together.

Trying to get along in a world that treated them as strange.

Ralph flew in circles, laughing with his friend Petunia. They shrieked as they circled one another and pushed their paws off against the shining white walls.

Petunia was a stripy black and tawny kitten to Ralph's gray.

And he liked her very much.

Ralph had taken to bumping his head against Petunias and asking her to fly again and again. More often than he asked anybody else. They often curled up together at night at the edge of the huddle of the other kittens.

Ralph had strange feelings for Petunia, but he

didn't know what they meant. All he knew was that he wanted to be near her.

A white coat came into the room and grabbed Ralph from the air. He shrieked and Petunia cried out his name before scrambling to land.

Ralph fought against the rougher-than-usual grip of the human's hands.

"You're up next, buddy," the white coat said. "Time for the old snip snip."

Ralph didn't know what the old snip snip was, but it doesn't sound good. He fought harder, scratching at a hand, and got a clout against the head which stunned him temporarily.

Ralph kicked his little hind feet, and the white coat gripped the scruff of Ralph's neck, making him submit.

"Dammit. You couldn't make this easy could you? Calm down little buddy. You won't feel a thing."

As the big metal door clanged behind them, Ralph heard Petunia call his name.

I t didn't take long at all to formulate a plan that led a small pride of six comrades to the slight, wooded rise just beyond the parking lot of a long, low building that squatted like a metallic toad beneath them.

Once Bruiser got an idea in her head, the rest of

the freehold pretty quickly figured out a way to get it done.

Besides, they were used to these sorts of operations. It was what they were known for: rescuing cats in need. There were cats in the compound who had been saved from fires and floods, from strange humans who crammed too many cats into too small a space, from beatings, from abandonment at roadsides...and from cages of all kinds.

Other cats whispered stories about a shadowy group of superhero cats they called The Liberators. They were talking about this compound, whether they knew it or not.

All cats weren't superheroes, but some superheroes were cats. And it was a superhero's job to help where they could. Otherwise, what was the use?

But the cats of the compound did not call themselves anything other than Free Cats. And that was what they wished for every cat living in misery. Simple freedom.

So, Bruiser, Hemingway, Pipsqueak and the others crouched outside the large ugly box of a human building. Pipsqueak had come from there most recently and didn't like to talk about it.

The little cat trembled slightly at Bruiser's side.

"You okay?" Bruiser growled.

"I'll be fine," Pipsqueak replied. And she would, Bruiser was certain of it.

Tom padded up. "The other two are in place by

the door, ready for us. All seems quiet enough. You're sure the humans aren't in the kitten room?"

Bruiser closed her eyes to check again. She saw humans in white coats gathered around a table, eating food. There were others in a different long room, peering at glowing machines.

She opened her eyes and stared at the marmalade cat. "The kitten room is clear."

Then she turned to Hemingway. "Go ahead. If you need help with any locks, I can try to teleport the screws or latches, but I think your paws should suffice."

Then she looked from cat to cat. "Remember, trust your instincts and trust each other."

Hemingway and Tom ran lightly back down towards the back door of the building, with Bruiser and Pipsqueak following several cat-length's behind. Bruiser's heart pounded in her chest. It didn't matter how many operations the crew successfully pulled off...

This could always be the one that didn't work.

This could always be the one where someone got injured, died, or worse.

Got captured.

Ralph's stomach didn't feel right, and his head was woozy. He blinked his eyes and the bars of the cage enclosure wavered in and out of focus.

Where was he? Why wasn't he in the big blanket pile with the other kittens?

And then he remembered.

The white coats. A strange, sweet, scent, and then darkness.

"Ralph?" That was Petunia's voice, coming from somewhere beyond his cage.

"Ralph," she repeated, "are you okay?"

He struggled to sit up, but his stomach heaved in protest. Ralph gave a mewling groan.

"He doesn't sound so good." That was Fee, another one of the litter.

"What should we do?" Another familiar voice spoke, but Ralph was too tired to figure out who.

"I've seen this before, it happens."

That was Mother's warm voice. Oh, she wasn't the one who had given birth to them, just as the rest of the litter weren't Ralph's real brothers and sisters, but she was the adult cat who took care of them, they all called her Mother just the same.

"They take them away and cut off their little balls," she said.

"No!" Toby said.

"Really?" Petunia squeaked.

"Yes. It means they don't want you to breed more

kittens. It's a terrible, terrible, thing," Mother continued. "But it is our lot in life."

A thought struggled to surface in the back of Ralph's head. A mild protest at Mother's words. How could this be his lot in life?

He was a cat who could fly.

Hemingway got the outside door open, with only a small amount of help from Bruiser. The six cats skulked into the overly bright corridor, lined with doors. Bruiser wrinkled her nose at the harsh scents that filled the air.

"Which way?" Tom asked.

Bruiser paused. Tried to listen past the low humming of the lights and the soft hissing and whirring sounds that came from behind closed doors. She heard human laughter further on, but before that noise...

"The kittens are in the third door to the right. I can smell them."

She could also hear some low, distressed meows. She only hoped they were not too late.

Bruiser whispered, "Hemingway, you work the latch. Celeste and Tom, be ready to pounce. Tortoise? You and I will get the lay of the land. I saw blanket boxes and but there are cages in there, too. I'm not sure at this point how many are locked up, so we'll need to make decisions as we go. Follow my lead if you can. If humans come? We all know what to do."

She turned to the littlest member of their squad. "Pipsqueak?"

The little cat snapped her head to attention.

"It is your job to reassure any cat who is afraid." Bruiser looked into the kitten's green eyes. "They will trust you."

Pipsqueak dipped her head in acknowledgement.

"Let's do this," Bruiser said.

"**D**rink some water, youngling," Mother said.

Ralph swung his head and saw a metal water dish. He looked at it through blurry eyes. He *was* thirsty, but his stomach still felt wrong.

"It will clear the poison out faster," Mother said. "That is what happened to the others. The sick feeling goes away more quickly."

Ralph scooted toward the dish and obediently lapped up some of the cool liquid. When nothing bad happened, he lapped up some more.

As he drank, a rattling started at the door. Ralph froze. Were the white coats back again?

The door opened with a burst, and six shapes barreled through, low to the ground. Not white coats.

Cats.

One shape took to the air. Another flyer! Ralph

drank more water, trying to clear his head. This was all so exciting! Nothing like this had ever happened before!

"Ralph!" Petunia flew up to the cage so he could see her little face. His eyesight must be clearing. She looked beautiful. "Two cats are going to open up your cage. Stay back from the door!"

Then she disappeared replaced by a noble gray face that just cleared the bottom of the cage. "I'm going to help you, son."

Two great paws reached for the latch. Were those six toes? And how could the cat bend them that way?

The cat looked down. "I'll need your help to lift the latch."

Ralph heard a steady voice answer, and then his stomach lurched again. Something weird was happening. The latch rattled, but focusing on that made his head go funny, so he looked out past the bars. Cats were running everywhere, and the flying ones swooped and dodged. It looked like some cats were escaping the room!

"Petunia!" he called for his friend. She flew into view again.

"Don't worry, Ralph. They are here to rescue us! These cats will set us free!"

He heard humans shouting down the hall. Petunia lurched in alarm.

Ralph heard the latch snick free.

"Come along, son." The gray-faced, six-toed cat

swung the cage door open. "Do you need help getting out?"

Ralph stood just as two white coats burst into the room. He was still a little woozy.

"I don't think I can fly."

"Can you jump onto my back?" The other cat spoke. She was large and solid looking, with a fierce gaze.

"I... I think so."

"Then jump on. We're out of time."

He could see that. Petunia and the other flying cats raced toward the white coats, claws extended like tiny rows of knives.

Human voices bellowed, cats hissed and yelled.

Ralph crouched, closed his eyes, and leapt.

Luckily, the kitten made it. Bruiser winced as his small claws dug through her fur.

"Hold on!" she said. "Hemingway! Run interference!"

The big gray cat barreled toward the thicket of human legs and fighting cats, creating a small opening. Bruiser imagined herself a small projectile, as if she could teleport herself and her small charge through that space and out of the building.

It worked. Soon enough, she followed the stream of paws and fur, racing down the hallway to the open door. Sunshine glowed at the end of the corridor.

Without a thought, Bruiser followed Hemingway toward the glowing rectangle, focused only on that space.

She trusted her comrades to take care of the rest. Tortoise and Celeste would see it through.

And Pipsqueak? Bruiser just had to hope the little cat's brave heart would keep her safe.

Humans shouted behind her, and she felt a whoosh of displaced air as if a large hand grabbed for her tail.

Bruiser put on speed and barreled toward the light.

Ralph couldn't believe it.

He was free.

Oh, he'd lost the contents of his stomach after lurching off the big cat's back once they'd reached a nice little place filled with good smells and things called trees and bushes, with intriguing flying creatures darting in and out. They had feathers instead of fur, and there were a lot of them.

But Ralph had been able to climb back onto Bruiser's back, and held on happily until they reached what the other cats called "the freehold."

He was curled up with Petunia on a soft cushion

in a vast human-building that smelled nothing like the lab. The light here was soft, not harsh. And there were cats everywhere.

"Are we in heaven?" he asked Petunia, before his eyes shuttered again. He'd been drifting in and out of sleep ever since they arrived. He couldn't help it.

Mother said it might take a day for him to feel like himself again.

"You are not in heaven," a bass voice growled. That was the strong flier called Tortoise. He'd set himself to guard Ralph and Petunia's cushion. Ralph was glad. Tortoise made his heart feel safe.

"You are in the compound of the Free Cats. This is your new home, if you want it."

Petunia licked Ralph's ears. "Did you hear that, Ralph? Home."

"Home," he purred.

Then, snuggled next to the best kitten in the world, Ralph slipped back into sleep.

*W*ant more cats? Like cozy paranormal mysteries? Check out Rhiannon, Sarah, and their wacky friends in Seashell Cove.

T. THORN COYLE
AUTHOR OF THE WITCHES OF PORTLAND
BOOKSHOP WITCH
A SEASHELL COVE
PARANORMAL MYSTERY

ALSO BY T. THORN COYLE

FICTION

The Panther Chronicles (Complete)

To Raise a Clenched Fist to the Sky

To Wrest Our Bodies From the Fire

To Drown This Fury in the Sea

To Stand With Power on This Ground

The Witches of Portland (complete)

By Earth

By Flame

By Wind

By Sea

By Moon

By Sun

By Dusk

By Dark

By Witch's Mark

The Steel Clan Saga

We Seek No Kings

We Heed No Laws

We Ride at Night

Seashell Cove Paranormal Mysteries

Bookshop Witch

Haunted Witch

Tarot Witch

Running Witch

Short Story Collections

A Hint of Faery

A Touch of Faery

A Spark of Magic

A Flame for Yuletide

A Hope for Winter

A Speculation of Stars

A Speculation of Hope

Risk It All: Queer Stories of Love, Suspense, And Daring

Thresholds: Queer Stories of Love, Suspense, And Daring

Non-Fiction

Evolutionary Witchcraft

Kissing the Limitless

Make Magic of Your Life

Sigil Magic for Writers, Artists & Other Creatives

Crafting a Daily Practice

ABOUT THE AUTHOR

T. Thorn Coyle worked in several strange and diverse occupations before settling down into writing novels. Buy them a cup of tea and perhaps they'll tell you about it.

Author of the *Seashell Cove Paranormal Mystery* series, *The Steel Clan Saga*, *The Witches of Portland*, and *The Panther Chronicles*, Thorn's multiple non-fiction books include *Sigil Magic for Writers, Artists & Other Creatives*, and *Evolutionary Witchcraft*.

Thorn's work appears in many anthologies, magazines, and collections. They have taught magical practice in nine countries, on four continents, and in twenty-five states.

An interloper to the Pacific Northwest U.S., Thorn stalks city streets, writes in cafes, loves live music, and talks to crows, squirrels, and trees.

Connect with Thorn:
www.thorncoyle.com